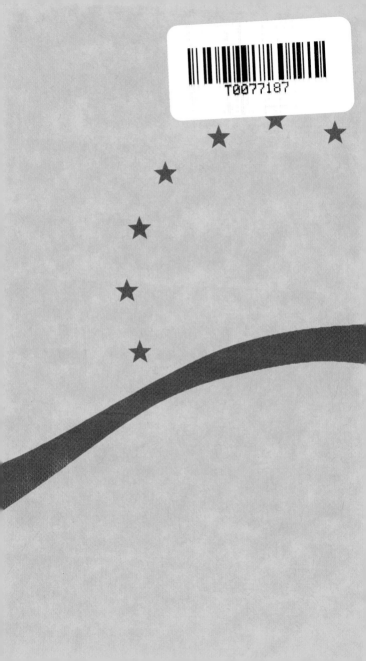

What Was Communism?

A SERIES EDITED BY TARIQ ALI

The theory of Communism as enunciated by Marx and Engels in *The Communist Manifesto* spoke the language of freedom, allied to reason. A freedom from exploitation in conditions that were being created by the dynamic expansion of capitalism so that 'all that is solid melts into air'. The system was creating its own grave-diggers. But capitalism survived. It was the regimes claiming loyalty to the teachings of Marx that collapsed and reinvented themselves. What went wrong?

This series of books explores the practice of twentieth-century Communism. Was the collapse inevitable? What actually happened in different parts of the world? And is there anything from that experience that can or should be rehabilitated? Why have so many heaven-stormers become submissive and gone over to the camp of reaction? With capitalism mired in a deep crisis, these questions become relevant once again. Marx's philosophy began to be regarded as a finely spun web of abstract and lofty arguments, but one that had failed the test of experience. Perhaps, some argued, it would have been better if his followers had remained idle dreamers and refrained from political activity. The Communist system lasted 70 years and failed only once. Capitalism has existed for over half a millennium and failed regularly. Why is one collapse considered the final and the other episodic? These are some of the questions explored in a variety of ways by writers from all over the globe, many living in countries that once considered themselves Communist states.

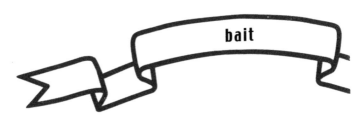
bait

four stories

MAHASWETA DEVI

TRANSLATED AND INTRODUCED
BY SUMANTA BANERJEE

Seagull
BOOKS

LONDON NEW YORK CALCUTTA

Seagull Books 2010

English language translation © Sumanta Banerjee 2005

ISBN-13   978 1 9064 9 749 1

British Library Cataloguing-in-Publication Data
A catalogue record for this book is available
from the British Library

Jacket and book designed by Sunandini Banerjee, Seagull Books
Printed at Leelabati Printers, Calcutta, India

Contents

Translator's Introduction

The plea that it is difficult to translate Mahasweta Devi's stories is an understatement. For anyone who has ever ventured into that exercise, it must have given the translator cramps! I am sure Mahasweta, being plainspoken herself, would not mind my indulging in that little bit of facetiousness to describe the awesome task that her stories demand from anyone trying to render them into a different language. The translator has to convey the suggestive sounds of the dialect that her tribal characters speak, the fire of the anguish and anger that her heroines breathe, the subtle nuances in her description of the Bengali political scenario where most of her stories take birth, the chilling asides while describing a murderous plot which may be hatched in a police station, and the devastating sarcasm that sears through the entire narrative.

When I was therefore requested to select and translate Mahasweta Devi's fiction, I chose to avoid the path trodden by my illustrious predecessors and opted instead for a few stories with which I personally felt comfortable. My comfort—if I may use the term—arises from my familiarity with the world she describes in these stories. It is the underworld of Calcutta and its suburbs in the decade between the 1960s and 1970s. I grew to acquire some knowledge of this violent but fascinating gangland in the course of the various roles that I played during those tumultuous years. To start with, as a reporter for *The Statesman* with crime as my beat for some time in the early 1960s, I had the opportunity of meeting some of the veterans of the Calcutta underworld of the past. Later, in the mid 1970s, when I spent some time during the Emergency as a Naxalite prisoner in Burdwan jail, I discovered amongst my jail mates a new and different breed of Bengali dacoits and gang lords. Talking to them, I was struck by the transformation that had taken place in the Bengali underworld in the decade between 1960 and 1970, one which could provide an important clue to changes in the Bengali social psyche as well as to developments in the West Bengal political scene which was getting increasingly criminalized.

I could gauge how the police–criminal– politician axis had evolved into a powerful institution to an extent unknown in the past. The police in particular had become a major arm of this axis— manipulating the criminal gangs or eliminating them, according to the interests of their political party bosses. It is these sociopolitical trends in the contemporary Bengali gangland which are captured by Mahasweta Devi in these stories. A variety of characters—inhabitants of a dangerous and oppressive underworld—surreptitious, moving from one place to another, killing and being killed, and all for no reason other than the sport of rival politicians. The new gods, for whom these miserable souls are 'as flies to wanton boys'.

Incidentally, the modern Bengali underworld has a long history, one that can be traced back to the 1940s. By using the adjective 'modern', I am drawing a barrier between the nature and organization of criminal activities in Bengal before the outbreak of the Second World War, and those that followed it. The outbreak was a watershed. The War economy modernized the underworld by carving out new areas of crime and encouraging the participants to evolve new methods. During the War, Calcutta became the headquarters of the South East Asia Command which brought in its trail hundreds of American and British soldiers. This opened up an avenue for a new generation of underworld operators. The devastating famine of 1943 that hit Bengal during the War (caused primarily by the diversion of foodgrains by the British administration to feed

the armed forces, and gross profiteering by unscrupulous Indian businessmen over the distribution
of whatever little was left), forced starving families
from the countryside to come to Calcutta. Their
women became victims of underworld operators
who supplied them to the British and American soldiers. Hoarding of scarce foodgrains and selling
them on the black market became another thriving
business for landlords and traders. They all needed
the help of muscle-men to further their interests and
protect their gains. These mercenaries were recruited from the underworld and later emerged as a
powerful and organized force, continuing to play a
major role in Bengali society and politics even after
the end of the famine and the War.

As the War came to a close, the foreign troops
departed. But they left behind a huge arsenal of
arms that found their way into the dens of the underworld mobsters. Guns began to rule the roost;
they were put to use with ferocious intensity by the
gang lords in 1946 when communal riots broke out
between Hindus and Muslims in Calcutta and other

places. The riots brought about a shift in the attitude of society towards these gang lords or goondas. With the police force totally dysfunctional in the riot-affected localities, ordinary citizens, both Hindus and Muslims, sought protection from the goondas of their respective communities, in order to save their lives and properties from attacks by marauders. These goondas became local heroes. But their acts no longer remained confined to self-defence or protection only. They satisfied the popular lust for avenging murders and for retaliating against the abduction of women of one community by gangsters of another, by re-enacting mirror-images of violence. Goondas indiscriminately killing innocent people or raping women of the 'enemy' began to acquire a social sanction among members of that community.

But these trends in the underworld activities during the 1946 Hindu–Muslim riots were not mere expressions of revenge. They revealed deeper political manipulations. In fact, the 1946 riots were a well-planned violence orchestrated by two contending political forces competing for power in post-World War India. The gangsters who led the riots were patronized by the politicians. Among Muslims, Mina Peshawari was one such character who was reported to be close to Hussain Shaheed Suhrawardy, the Muslim League Chief Minister of Bengal in those days. Similarly, the Hindus found a saviour in Gopal Mukherjee (more familiarly known as Gopal Pantha, since he used to run a butcher's shop selling goat meat—*pantha* in Bengali—in Bowbazar, Calcutta), patronized by the Hindu Congress politicians. The politician–underworld nexus that Mahasweta Devi describes in her stories of the present days can thus claim a long ancestry.

It was many years later, in the 1960s—when as a reporter I was investigating Calcutta's underworld—that I met Gopal Pantha in a makeshift temple on Ganesh Avenue near its crossing at Wellington Square. By then he had become a religious devotee of sorts and with his flowing beard, looked like a saint. Although Gopal-da (as he was fondly addressed by his admirers and neighbours) appeared to be reluctant to narrate his exploits of the days of the 1946 riots, his followers who surrounded him—some among them his old comrades-in-arms—proudly told me how he and his 'boys' had set up defence squads in the Bowbazar–College Street area to protect the Hindu inhabitants from attack by Muslim goondas. When reminded of allegations that his 'boys' also butchered innocent Muslims and raped Muslim women, most of them vehemently denied it, while a few others shrugged off the accusation saying that such things were bound to happen in those surcharged days!

Manipulating memories of murderous acts either by erasing them altogether or blunting their uncomfortable jarring edges by a sort of rationalization is a familiar tendency among the underworld veterans. I have found it often when talking to a later generation of desperados. Mahasweta Devi brilliantly captures this tension in the nest of one's personal memories in her story 'Killer' (*Ghatok* in the Bengali original), while describing the retrospection that the young assassin goes through during his return journey to Calcutta.

The 1950–60 period saw the flowering of the politician–underworld nexus in West Bengal in its full bloom. A new class of gangsters, known as *mastaans*, appeared on the streets of Calcutta and its suburbs. The leaders of the ruling Congress party picked them up as muscle-men to beat up activists of Opposition parties and to threaten their followers at election time. Leading among such protégés of the Congress party whom I remember were dreaded mobsters like Phata Kesto of College Street, Bhanu and Jaga(nnath) in the Wellington Square neighbourhood, and Inu Mitra of Baranagar. Their gangs sometimes went beyond their political brief of knocking out anti-Congress party activists, their political clout allowing them to terrorize the common citizens of their respective areas by extorting protection money from shopkeepers or carrying away young girls whom they fancied. Protected by the local ruling-party bosses who were usually legislators or municipal councillors, these gangs of *mastaan*s could cock a snook at the police or bribe them to, quite literally, get away with murder. It was thus that the politician–gangster–police troika became institutionalized in West Bengal, and continues to hold sway even today under a Left Front regime.

The troika received a boost in the decade of the 1960s and 1970s when the ruling politicians and the administration sought the help of the underworld to destroy the Naxalite movement and eliminate its peasant and student cadres who posed an armed challenge to the Establishment with their pro-gramme of putting an end to feudal and capitalist oppression.

Bengali middle-class society in the meantime had undergone a sea change. The underworld had emerged from its hitherto subterranean location to occupy the open environs of Bengali middle-class homes. Hundreds of unemployed youth from such homes, most of them educated, had drifted into the underworld during this period mainly to make a fast buck. Patronage by established political leaders who hired them to carry out their dirty work not only yielded them cash but also assured them protection from the law as well as a certain status in local soci-ety. In the process, they transmitted the criminal values and norms of the underworld into their homes. Dacoities and extortions, lootings and killings, hitherto looked down upon by the respectable middle-class families as crimes committed by professional goondas and the scum of the lower classes, now began to be grudgingly accepted by many of these families as the only desperate means available to their unemployed sons who could thus provide them with food and shelter. Mahasweta Devi's novel *Murderer-er Ma* (The Murderer's Mother) gives us an intimate picture of the tragic depths of degeneration and criminalization to which such Bengali families were forced to descend.

In order to seek protection for their anti-social means of livelihood, these young desperados yoked themselves to some political boss or other. Their professional expertise turned out to be an asset for these politicians who employed them as hit men to bump off their rivals. This abundant reservoir of Bengali middle-class lumpen mercenaries came in handy for the West Bengal police when they launched their operations against the Naxalite cadres. The administration supplemented direct police onslaught on these cadres with the recruitment of local young Bengali middle-class hit men who were deployed to finish off known Naxalites in their respective localities. In a more Machiavellian move, the police made them infiltrate into the Naxalite ranks and kill their leading members at an opportune moment, taking advantage of the internecine disputes that tore the movement apart.

This anti-Naxalite strategy inaugurated a phase that saw the elimination of an entire generation of young people, and the brutalization of those who survived, through inter-gang rivalries and fratricidal killings—partly motivated by political ambitions and partly manipulated by the police administration.

The spectre of the ruthless anti-Naxalite offensive launched by the police in those days looms large over the tersely narrated story 'Fisherman' (*Dheebar* in the Bengali original). Here again, Mahasweta makes no mention of the Naxalites. But to any Bengali reader familiar with the decade of the 1970s, it would be obvious from her subtle suggestive notes that the bodies dumped into the tank by the police were of those young boys suspected of political affiliation to the Naxalite movement, 'more dangerous than the tigers of the forest, more dangerous than the snakes in their holes'. It was a common practice with the police in those days to round up young boys in cities or villages, and surreptitiously kill them if they were suspected of any Naxalite connections, and then dispose of their bodies in some distant place to pass off their killings as cases of unaccounted murder. In Calcutta, the blind lanes and alleys provided the police with ideal spots for dumping these bodies. In the villages, the tanks were the dumping spots, as described meticulously by Mahasweta.

Another story, 'Knife' (*Chhuri* in the Bengali original), is a splendid tongue-in-cheek account of gang warfare in a suburban town of West Bengal, bordering Bangladesh. But the period in which she locates the story is no longer the politically volatile decade of 1960–70. The Naxalites have been finished off and their killers are now ruling the roost.

The gang lords are now demanding their pound of flesh for having done the dirty job on behalf of their political patrons and the police. Armed with enough fire-power, they have emerged as a hegemonic force in society.

Published first in 1985 (in the Bengali magazine *Anushtup*), the story 'Knife' evokes intimately the ambience of the daily life of such a society in contemporary West Bengal. Even though ruled by the Left Front, it has not made any difference to the operations of the underworld that continue to thrive with the help of the local police and politicians. Smugglers, mafia dons, hired killers, religious charlatans, political leaders of various hues ranging from the tricolour to the red, police officers—all the small town knaves and gangsters crowd here in a rollicking murderous carnival, to the music of bomb blasts and slogan shouting. Mahasweta Devi has an eye for the colours of the environs where they live and operate, as well as an ear for their racy slang and the names that they invent for their dons.

Like the special slang of the underworld, distinctive pseudonyms and titles are reserved for its dons who either baptize themselves or are christened by their followers with exotic or spine-chilling aliases. These are either borrowed from some distinct identification marks left on their bodies in the course of their operations, or better still, from their expertise in certain fields of operation. Thus, in the 1950s, I heard of a gangster in south Calcutta who was known as Hat-kata Bachchu ('Bachchu without a hand', which he lost while exploding a bomb). He was soon overtaken by Bomabaj Ganesh ('Ganesh, the expert bomb-thrower')! Another *mastaan* assumed the name Hitler! Our modern political historians need not rack their brains to discover any Nazi connection. This small-time operator, to elevate his status in his locality, was only picking up the name of an international figure who had inspired awe and fear all around the world!

Mahasweta's use of the lexicon of the Bengali underworld and its nomenclature, is firmly grounded on a perfect knowledge of the ways and habits of its inhabitants and how they spread their tentacles. In 'Knife', she describes life in a mofussil town, where the underworld has not only come out in the open, but dominates society. Its slang has become a part of the vocabulary of its inhabitants, and its gang lords, the rulers of their destiny. The narrative can be examined as an excellent example of [Antonio] Gramsci's concept of hegemony in civil society—by the criminal underworld, in this case, instead of his cherished proletariat! The gang lords are household names in the town. Their names sometimes sound exotic, sometimes reverential, sometimes fearful—Germany, Sachcha (which incidentally means 'honest'!), Baba, Paolan (a self-styled distortion of the world *palowan* which means wrestler?). They are no longer denigrated as goondas—the old derogatory Bengali term—but elevated by the euphemistic term *controllers*.

They are not figments of Mahasweta's imagination. We can recognize them as actual people who stride across the present Bengali social scene. Let me give an example. In one sequence of 'Knife', the local citizens' committee when trying to mobilize the residents for a meeting to protest against the atrocities of the gang lords of the area, make the announcement: 'Gauribari has shown the way. Anantapur will not lag behind!' The allusion is to an actual happening in a place called Gauriber or Gauribari, in Ultadanga on the north-eastern fringes of Calcutta in the 1980s, where the residents rose in revolt against a local don called Hemen Mandal, and drove him out from the area. At the peak of his power, in November 1979, Hemen Mandal gave a candid interview to a Bengali newspaper, which sheds light on the growth and rise of a typical urban gang lord in West Bengal today.

It is worth quoting excerpts from the interview, even if they are long, for an understanding of the psyche of the underworld characters whom Mahasweta Devi portrays. Tracing his life story, Hemen said, I got involved in fighting in this locality, first in 1967, over rivalry in sports. Before that I was Hemen Mandal, like any other ordinary boy of Gauriber. But all of a sudden, I found our rivals attacking us with the help of goondas. Should we lose to them? I also gathered together a number of boys and formed a gang. I was then fifteen or sixteen years old. Whenever our opponents came to attack us, we resisted. From such *West Side Story*-like youthful gang fights, Hemen soon graduated into a full-fledged goonda. In his own words, With every passing day, I moved further ahead of my gang—further and further . . . I began to make bombs and use them. As I moved ahead, a time came when even I myself could not remember when and how I had become a goonda . . .

But till the late 1960s, Hemen remained a mere local goonda, preventing rival gangs from occupying his territory in Gauriber. Neither did he have any political leanings, nor did he seek protection from any political leader. It was this lapse on his part that cost him dearly. He was an orphan-like character in the underworld of the late 1960s, when most of the seniors in his peer group had already been recruited by some political party or other and were thus well-protected from police persecution. Bereft of such protection, Hemen soon fell foul of the police. To escape their dragnet, he went underground in 1969 and managed to lie low till 1972, when he was arrested. He remained in jail till his release in 1975.

After his release, Hemen realized the need for political patronage for his future career as a *mastaan*. Coming out from jail in 1975, Hemen said in his interview, I got involved in Congress politics. He chose to ally with one faction of the Congress party headed by a leader who still remains an important luminary in West Bengal politics. But Hemen made it clear in the interview that his alliance was part of a bargain. In exchange for the protection provided by his political patron, he was willing to supply him with his muscle-power. The muscle-power was made up of his 'boys' whom he proudly described as future politicians: These boys will join politics in future. I'm keeping them in my fold from now on . . . They are in charge of keeping my territory under my control. I'll decide which politician I'll support. They (the politicians) will have to approach me . . . But in defence of this Godfather-like bravado, Hemen soon apologetically added, Everyone is behaving like that!

It is this sociopolitical model of living where everyone behaves 'like that' ('that' being the pattern of a totally unscrupulous lifestyle ranging from cheating and thieving to murdering and mass killing), and which is adopted by our society, that is uncovered and mercilessly dissected by Mahasweta Devi in her stories. The *mastaans* in 'Knife' even incorporate current political rhetoric into their slang and stamp them with new meanings. Thus, they believe in 'freedom' and 'struggle'. As for 'freedom', the black marketeers . . . should be given the 'freedom' to carry on their business as long as the *controllers* get their regular commission from them . . . they also believe in the need for carrying on the 'struggle'. Their 'struggle' is for capturing orbits of control and chunks of business. And in this 'struggle' of theirs, they can invariably depend on the protection of the thana-babu—the local police sub-inspector who always hovers around in Mahasweta Devi's stories of the underworld. Her cold and pungent style of narration is reminiscent of Dashiel Hammett, the suburban town of West Bengal where she locates her story like a modern Bengali counterpart of the American town Personville (renamed by its inhabitants as Poisonville because of its gangsters) in Hammett's immortal novel *Red Harvest*.

Surely the goons of today's West Bengal do not need to learn new lessons from their predecessors in the USA of the 1920s, the gangsters of Hammett's novels. But they share the same instincts and behaviour that cut across borders of time and space. It is these that bind together the underworld of Mahasweta's contemporary West Bengal and that of Dashiel Hammett's in the USA of the 1920s. It is a universal and lasting solidarity that has proved to be more powerful in its impact on society than the message of working-class solidarity that was once offered by a now-forgotten German philosopher way back in the nineteenth century.

Although used as sidekicks in the modern underworld of West Bengal, women can often play an independent role. An old madam of Malati's generation in 'Knife' for instance, receives and hides stolen goods, provides shelter to gangsters on the run and acts as a conduit between them and the police. But she is adroit enough to bring about the downfall of a powerful gang lord like Germany. While madams like Malati continue to dominate the sleazy nooks and corners of the underworld, a new class of call-girls has appeared on its upper levels who do business with the higher-ups in metropolitan society. Unlike the loud haggling and brawls in the murky slums, their mode of operation is quiet and unobtrusive, subtle and sophisticated.

Mahasweta selects one such girl as her heroine in 'Body' (*Shareer* in the Bengali original). In keeping with the silent nature of this girl's functioning, Mahasweta chooses a cryptic style to narrate her story. Extremely condensed, the story packs a host of vignettes of criminal activities that take place beneath the calm and gentle surface of Calcutta's social exterior. The girl—her name is Ketaki, but all along she is described as 'the girl'—was orphaned as a child when her tribal parents were hanged for committing murders. She grew up in a state-run institution and studied in a college but drifted into the profession of stealing. Once when she was caught, she was rescued from the police station by a man called M (a procurer?), who supplied her to a politician whose name is Nripati, meaning 'Emperor', a name he lives up to. These are the only skeletal nuggets of information that Mahasweta supplies us about her heroine.

In Mahasweta Devi's story 'Draupadi' (translated into English earlier), the tribal Naxalite heroine Dopdi, after being gangraped by the minions of the law, overcomes her humiliation by standing naked before their senior police officer, laughing and spitting blood at him, and pushing him with her two mangled breasts—making him afraid for the first time of an unarmed target. In 'Body', the heroine is ravished and used by the makers of the law—a politician and his cohorts. Both Dopdi and she are victims of the predatory male Establishment. Incidentally, both are of tribal origins. Yet, the girl fails to take revenge—both for her own humiliation and for the capture of her beloved.

Unlike Dopdi who was a political activist fighting against the oppressors, this girl was being used as a secret agent, her only asset being her body. Was her final decision—to destroy her body—the ultimate form of her protest against a patriarchal Establishment?

AS HER READERSHIP IS FULLY AWARE, whether Mahasweta Devi writes a short story, a novel, a play or a political article, she manages to convey the extraordinary relish that she has for her medium. Her non-Bengali readers are, by now, familiar with her work, thanks to a number of translations of several writings that have come out during the last decade or so. They reveal the wide spectrum of her narrative genius. Her characters range from historical figures of our anti-colonial struggles to present day rebels against an oppressive political Establishment; from modern India's marginalized rural communities like tribals and dalits to Bengali middle-class families fighting desperately to escape marginalization in today's society. In her fiction, gender exploitation cuts across class barriers, embracing girls from poorer classes who are victims of a male predatory socio-economic order, as well as housewives of middle-class homes who are harassed by a patriarchal domestic order. The issue of motherhood, which comes up in several of her stories and novels, is not confined to a critique of the male exploitation of the submissive woman (as a tool for procreation), but extends to the portrayal of the mother as a rebel asserting her rights. *Hajar Churashir Ma* (translated as *Mother of 1084*) is a lasting testimony to Mahasweta's acute and sensitive understanding of the traumatic state of anxiety that mothers of young boys in West Bengal had to undergo in those terrifying days of the anti-Naxalite persecution campaign that the police launched in the 1970s.

While scripting the story of the exploitation and oppression that these characters suffer, she never forgets to underscore their attempts at resistance— sometimes violent, sometimes quiet, sometimes even crafty in their wily efforts to outwit their powerful enemies. To describe this relentless struggle between the oppressed and the oppressors, the powerful and the powerless, at the various levels of our society, Mahasweta Devi has developed a unique style that combines stinging wit with a note of pathos. When she touches this note in her stories, it never degenerates into the melodrama that is the usual staple of most bestsellers by today's Bengali authors. Instead, it gains force from the contrast with the tone of un-emotional cynicism with which she narrates the events or describes the characters.

Mahasweta Devi is at her acerbic best in the four stories that make up this collection. They also provide the reader with a different facet of Mahasweta Devi's oeuvre. Unlike the tribal rebels, or Naxalite revolutionaries, or marginalized women, who dominate her world of fiction, the characters in these stories are denizens of the criminal under-world. They stand midway between the oppressors and those who resist them. They are the tools used by the former to punish or eliminate the latter. These agents of the enemy camp form a lively cloak-and-dagger world, attracting all the gusto of Mahasweta's literary creativity. True to her passion for observing and recording the minutest details in the behaviour of people around her, she discovers and depicts the various tendrils that climb up along the multi-curvilinear Bengali underworld. Among the icy peaks of her cold cynical narrative of this Bengali underworld, there suddenly appear the lightning flashes of brief moments that suggest her sympathy for these loners. But her vision is harsh. There is no false comfort for these youngsters. They are doomed to a destiny that is reserved for them.

The people described in these stories are the children of a new age of crime. They are freed from the last vestiges of moral scruples, and emancipated by a new political order that hires them as killers and provides them with all immunity from prosecution. It is an age where the advance of political chicanery allows financing of crime as never before. It is done through organized smuggling, state-sponsored corruption and nepotism, extortion and racketeering by elected legislators on a grand scale. Patronized by politicians, protected by the police and equipped with all the modern technical resources of murder, these gangsters straddle both the underworld of the criminals and the world of the respectable gentry—forging a kinship of intrigue that has become very much a part of the modern Bengali society.

It is these hoodlums and desperados, the derelicts and drifters of the Bengali underworld as well as their political patrons and protectors in the police, whom Mahasweta brings to life with her caustic pen in the pages of these stories. As she pillories the respectable representatives of power in our political system who sustain this underworld, she offers us the extraordinary chance to watch a lifelike effigy of the bizarre structure of Indian democracy burning in the background.

I

Fisherman

The man owns a net. At one time, when people dredged the tank for weeds, caught fish, cleared away the water-hyacinths, he used to cast his net over the water.

He'd cast his net and catch fish in the master's tank. But the master no longer bred fish there.

Jagat's net now just hangs in his room. When anyone asks for it, he rents it out.

Jagat has found other work, now. Now, every other day, he's summoned by the local police.

Jagat, you there?

Yes, sir.

You'll have to come, once.

Where, sir?

Raypukur.

The bastards choose Raypukur every time!

Jagat puts on black underpants. Slathers his body with oil. Picks up a long bamboo pole. The tank is surrounded by the police. A dom[1] stands, waiting. And a sheet of tarpaulin stretched out on the bank. Jagat first takes a bidi[2] from the dom, takes a few long drags. Then dives into the water.

In the past, incredible wonders had lain submerged, hidden deep in these waters of the Raypukur. Men had dived in to emerge again with priceless vessels, vessels used for worshipping the

gods. It was rumoured that many people had discovered jewellery, gold coins, other treasures.

But the waters of Raypukur now conceal a different wonder. Jagat dives deep, then opens his eyes.
Greenish, murky water. The frightened *techokho*[3] fish
move away. The shrimps dart about, their feelers
waving, dancing. Earlier, Jagat would poke about
with his bamboo pole to discern the correct spot.

Now, he no longer needs to prod the depths.
Way below the surface, flat upon the mud, stretched
out on its back, lies the body. Around it, the bubbles
that rise in unsteady columns. Ever so carefully, Jagat
tugs at a leg. Sometimes, the hands. Then he sur-
faces, breathes for a while, fills his lungs with air.

Found him, Jagat?

Where can he go?

Jagat retrieves the body with the greatest of
care. As it breaks through the surface, its silent
protest poisons the air; the stench of rotting flesh
carries quickly on the breeze. Jagat lays it down
upon the tarpaulin. Then he scrubs at his arms,

scouring them from the wrists up to the elbows, with mud from the tank.

These days Jagat demands seven rupees per corpse. What, after all, is the value of a rupee today? The value of money, the price of human lives, both so cheap these days. Jagat is certain that those who kill get money. Jagat can't believe that anything is possible without money.

He believes that the dom—constables—police inspector, the murderer and the murdered, are all part of one enormous cash transaction.

When Jagat talks like this, his son says, Foolish man! But this son of his, Abhay, despite his *technical school* education, never explains why it is Jagat who is foolish, and Abhay who is clever.

Then Jagat comes back home. Washes his hands and legs with *carbolic* soap. Then goes off to collect the money.

This place is on the outskirts. This place is described in the old deed of the Ray family as 'a sacred spot of mango orchards and paddy fields, washed by the waters of the Ganga'.

The Ganga now dwindled, a silted-up creek. The orchards now bereft of mango trees. The paddy fields now inhabited by human beings. And not an inch of the 'sacred spot' remains under the control of the family. The memory of the Rays lives on only in the names—the place, Raybagan, and the tank, Raypukur.

It helps to be on the outskirts. Even if there's a murder, no one makes a noise. No parents come to the police station or the morgue in search of their sons. What amazes Jagat is that no one even weeps aloud in grief these days.

Jagat realizes that the world is becoming loveless. The youth, without any compassion. And even the parents no longer allow any cries of sorrow to escape their lips.

And yet, Jagat had heard that affection was downward-flowing, spontaneously streaming from the elders to the young ones. For as a child, Jagat's uncle would take him across the Ganga. On its banks there was a camp of political prisoners. One among them, an old man, would read the Ramayana in the evenings. Jagat's uncle and his friends would sit and listen whenever they had some time to spare.

Jagat too would listen to the tales of greatness. He learnt that love and affection flowed down, naturally, from the old to the young, from parent to child, he learnt that even if the son forgot his mother, the mother never forgot her son.

But now sitting in Raybagan, who remembers all that? He has learnt now to tell himself that no one was murdered here. Only a few boys, once in a while, from this locality or that, just disappear.

And then Jagat is summoned.

For, the last resort of all those boys is the bottom of the tank. Jagat has been told that these boys are more dangerous than tigers in the forest, more deadly than snakes in their holes.

Jagat agrees that they are dangerous. No matter how innocent your faces, how young you look, I know how dangerous you really are! Or else, why die like this?

Jagat doesn't want to think, doesn't want to delve too deep. He collects his seven rupees and gives five to his wife Bhamini. Then, two rupees in hand, he goes off to get drunk.

His only eccentricity, his one uncivilized habit.

Abhay asks him, Why do you drink? Are you addicted?

Abhay is his son. Jagat's *technical school*-educated son, Abhay. When his father is sober, Abhay cannot talk to him, to that dark, grey-haired savage-looking man. Abhay cannot think of what to say. The man doesn't speak Abhay's language. The man, like a demon, that body, without any sense of shame. The man who introduces himself as, Jagat Sha, a fisherman by caste, sir!

Yet Abhay had escorted his father to court where his name was changed and registered as Jagat Chandra Das.

But Abhay and his father inhabit two different planets. Only when his father drinks does his gaze seem to mellow, his eyes blur with affection, with softness. It is no small sorrow for Abhay that he cannot speak to his father unless he is drunk.

Abhay asks him, Why do you drink? Are you addicted?

Addicted!

Then why don't you drink every day?

No, I don't.

Can't do without it when you've fished out a body?

No.

Jagat nods his head. Says, I feel so sad, Abhay. And so scared.

Scared?

Of people. How did things get this way?

Abhay leans against the door, stares out. His father is frightened of everyone, these days? And Abhay's mother? Perhaps she is only frightened of her son. Can they see the torment that scorches Abhay's soul?

But Abhay doesn't let them see, hasn't let them know. Abhay always speaks to them politely, calmly. Abhay is possessed of an immense affection for his father and his mother.

He asks his father, Baba, try not to drink one day after you've fished out a body.

I'm afraid, Abhay. Drink helps me forget for a bit.

Doesn't the water scare you, Baba?

No, Abhay.

Jagat smiles a little. These days he sometimes dives into the waters, swims through the depths. Just like that. Raypukur is an ancient tank. Standing at one end and looking across to the other side, how small the people look. In the monsoons, large rain-drops splatter off the green surface of the waters, like starbursts of light from sparklers that burn, white.

Jagat occasionally swims in the tank then, bathes there. He feels so close to the water then, so familiar, as though they were part of him. How tran-quil, how green is the world of water. How peaceful. The fish, the water snakes, the shrimps—snails—clams, the weeds and plants. So familiar, so very close to him.

Abhay, does it hurt a lot?

This is the time, when his father asks Abhay this usual question. And when Abhay realizes that he loves his father. Loves him very much. Wants to place his hand across his father's heart tenderly and let him know of that love.

Instead, Abhay asks, What, Baba?

Did I do you harm, by sending you to school?

Why harm, Baba?

Because you can't get a job, can't work . . . it must hurt.

Abhay does not reply.

You won't get any work the way you're trying. I'll make you *patnar*[4] in Mohan's workshop.

But he wants a lot of money.

So what? You think I'll never have enough?

Abhay becoming a *patnar* in Mohan's bicycle and cycle-rickshaw workshop has been Jagat's wish for a long time now.

But Baba, Mohan wants five to seven hundred rupees.

I'll give it, Abhay, I'll give. You carry on with
what you're doing.

Abhay smiles affectionately. Then leaves on his
bicycle.

Jagat lives in a large house in this locality. The
landowner lives abroad. It was he who had arranged
for these two rooms and the verandah in front to be
built for Jagat. The poultry coop had been built by
Jagat's wife Bhamini. She breeds hens and ducks.
Jagat takes their eggs to the market. This earns them
money throughout the year.

The nicer room is Abhay's. A chowki, a table, a
chair. Shirts, pyjamas, pants hanging on a line strung
across the room. A calendar on the wall. Sometimes
a glimpse of the room makes Jagat sigh. How Abhay
refused to marry. Refused to settle down with a girl
from their own community. Or else he'd have got a
small radio, a cycle-rickshaw from his father-in-law,
a little bit of cultivable land.

Abhay had said, Forget it! Abhay had laughed.
And Jagat had looked at Abhay, seen him for the

very first time. Tall, young, dark and yet not unattractive, Abhay. His face, that look, so composed.

Jagat had shaken his head. Even now he shakes his head, still bewildered. Why is Abhay a stranger to him? Had the times made him thus? And yet, ask him to lend a hand and this same boy will fix the fence, build the chicken coop, weed Bhamini's brinjal patch.

The boys these days, boys like him from homes just like theirs, sport new hairstyles, wear drainpipe trousers, strut about with transistors tucked under their arms. Go to the cinema. Their manner brash, their words rude.

Abhay is not like them. Who is Abhay like?

Jagat asks his wife, He's not like me, he's not like you. Then who's he like, my son? My only son?

You're a man and you don't know. How can I?

Bhamini doesn't talk much. Deep in her heart is an ache, a shaft of pain. She washes her son's clothes, cooks for him, but oh the sorrow of not being able to sit and share a word or two with him.

How Bhamini has run to Tarakeshwar come the full moon in Sraban.[5] Walking all the way, the pots of water so heavy on her shoulders. Abhay would go too, when he was a little boy.

Last year, Abhay said, Don't go anymore, Ma.

Why? Does it embarass you?

Their relatives had said to her, Can't you see, how ashamed he is of the two of you?

Abhay had laughed. If it means all that much to you, then go. But these are bad times, that's all.

Shall I go, then? You won't get angry?

Why should I?

So Bhamini went, a bamboo pole decorated with flowers balanced on one shoulder, a pot of water hanging from each end. On her way back, she bought sugar candy and a pumpkin from Tarakeshwar. But when she got home what did she see!

Abhay in the courtyard, talking to a girl and two boys.

My mother. Abhay said, pointing her out with a slight nod of his head. Bhamini thought she would never find the words to express her astonishment. How Abhay was speaking to them, just like an equal!

Since then, Bhamini has been treating Abhay with even more deference. But how strange has grown her son, dear heart, what a stranger he is to Bhamini. Bhamini can no longer imagine that this stranger-son will marry, bring home a wife, fill her home with the sound of squabbles–scoldings–love–tenderness, gift her household with little grandchildren.

She only asks of Jagat, Can't we send him away?

Why?

Everyone, is sending their young boys away, haven't you noticed?

Those're babu families, bhadraloks.[6]

Mention of words like babu–bhadralok makes Abhay say, No more of that, Baba.

Jagat feels frightened of his son, then. Such pain, as he drinks. Such sorrow, as he swims in the Raypukur. When did man grow to be so frightening?

Yet Daroga-babu, the dom, the doctor at the morgue—none of them frighten Jagat. How confident he is around them, how arrogantly he stands, how smartly he speaks. Daroga-babu sports a golden chain around his neck, a picture of Kali on the locket. When Jagat visits the police station, Daroga-babu says to Jagat, Your son's educated. Find him a job.

Please babu, can't you help?

It's not as if there aren't any jobs going. There are.

But where, babu?

Tell him to drop by.

Oh lord! But he's as timid as me!

Tell him, Give Daroga-babu some news every now and then, he'll pay. But look here, don't you go blabbing this all over the place now!

No, babu. But what sort of news?

Tell him. He'll know.

Abhay dismisses his father's words with a smile. Says, What news can I give him? Why doesn't he speak to Nrisingha Dutta instead? Persuade him to give me a job in the Corporation office? They're looking for people.

Who knows why this sensible suggestion makes Daroga-babu fly into a rage. He says, Wants a job, does he? Do jobs grow on trees, to be plucked at whim? Why? Didn't like my advice, didn't like the thought of getting cash in hand? I'm telling you Jagat, there's much suffering in store for you. Much suffering. And all you'll do is pull corpses out of the water and sell eggs in the market.

Jagat's son has passed out from a *technical school* whereas Daroga-babu's son only sells film tickets on the black market. Hence Daroga-babu nurses a secret grudge, a rage that simmers within. Jagat is not aware of this. Jagat does not understand.

So Jagat drags up corpses from the water, more corpses. How they must have run–jumped– frolicked–played–laughed. Dear lord! How Jagat fears people who are alive. And in the water now, see, how quiet, calm, still. Pressed down by stone slabs, weighed down by bricks. Their bodies now playgrounds for the fish.

The world that lies beneath is peaceful, green, mysterious. No starkness, no harsh outlines, nothing disturbs the eye. Not even the corpses. The little *techokho* fish, so beautiful, how their silver fins sparkle.

Jagat gets seven rupees per corpse. He gives five rupees to Bhamini. He spends the remaining two on drink. Drunk, Jagat stands by the door to Abhay's room.

It hurts a lot, doesn't it, Abhay?

Yes, Baba.

I know what hurts you, son. No work for you, yet you search high and low. That's why it hurts.

Baba . . . it's not looking for a job that . . .

There's something that Abhay wants to say. Yet he doesn't, he can't. A job! Is that all that hurts Abhay so? Baba dearest, how will you know what really hurts Abhay?

I know Abhay. How you yearn for work and yet, no luck. I'll make you a *patnar* at Mohan's.

How? Found hidden treasure? Or been stealing?

No, don't laugh, Abhay. Don't call your father a thief. I never steal. Daroga-babu has said he'll give me more work, more money.

Be careful of what he makes you do, Baba.

Why? Will he make trouble?

Baba, you don't understand anything. Why do you drink, Baba?

I'm scared, Abhay.

Scared?

Of people. So much sin, son! So many sinners!

Abhay smiles. A tender, serene smile. Regarding Jagat from a different, distant planet, smiling.

Abhay says, Come, let's eat now. Ma's served the rice already, she's waiting.

Jagat cannot refuse Abhay calling him thus. Jagat goes off to eat. But he cannot forget Daroga-babu's instructions. Come late at night, Jagat. There's work. And a lot of money.

It's the money that makes Jagat dive into Raypukur by the light of the full moon. But tonight, how

strange everything looks. Even familiar people be-
have in an unfamiliar way. Or else why should so
many people wait on the bank, even Daroga-babu?
Why that black van?

Jagat drags up the answers from the bottom of
the tank. Not one dive but six. Six bodies are
wrapped in tarpaulin by the police and bundled into
the van.

Daroga-babu gives him a lot of money that
night. Jagat has never seen so much cash in his life.
Daroga-babu warns him, Careful, Jagat! Not a word
about how many there were, or who. A peep out of
you and that's it.

Honest to God! Would I ever?

Their killers are ruthless, don't forget that
Jagat.

The pit of Jagat's belly turns to ice. Killers? But
they'd been arrested by the police! Taken to the
police station! After that? Jagat can't think any more,
doesn't want to think any more. He goes back home
and for the first time, doesn't drink.

But when Abhay is killed, it is not Jagat who drags up his body. Jagat never gets to know how Abhay was killed, or who killed him.

You called him to the police station only to ask some questions!

But didn't I release him? Ask everyone.

You let him go? Then when did you arrest him? Was I away at my sister's, in Dhabdhobi?

We wanted to find out where he goes, what sort of company he keeps. Once it was night we let him go.

Where?

Now go, Jagat! Stop whining.

Whining?

Yes.

My son's dead, no one left after me—don't I have the right to whine?

Daroga-babu drives him away.

Jagat returns home, weeping.

Then one day, Daroga-babu also disappears.

On his cycle, going back home. Nowhere to be found.

The police come to Jagat. Let's go, Jagat! Raypukur again.

Jagat stands on the bank of Raypukur, kicking at the broken bricks, the piles of cement.

Dive, Jagat! If Daroga-babu's corpse is found, be sure, all of Raypara will be a ground of corpses! The junior Daroga-babu roars aloud.

Jagat dives. All that lies beneath, so green, peaceful, dreamlike. Daroga-babu's body and his bicycle. Tied together with Abhay's *gamchha*.[7]

Jagat drags chunks of bricks, slabs of cement, piles them atop Daroga-babu's stomach. Let it be so, for now. Something else can be thought of in a day or two.

Jagat comes up for air.

Found him?

No.

Jagat answers, shaking his head. Then wipes dry his body, his hands, his legs. He must first send word to Bhamini, tell her to leave for his sister's at Dhabdhobi at once.

Did you look carefully?

I'm Jagat the fisherman, my lord. Have I ever been careless with your work? Sir?

Jagat's face crinkles as he smiles, an enigmatic smile. The junior Daroga-babu is astonished. Why is Jagat smiling? And how can he, so soon after the death of his son.

II

Knife

A dismal rainy evening. A small town in West Bengal. A district near the border. The shops that have sprouted up on either side of the main road, the slums behind them, the countless shanties that crowd around the railway tracks, suddenly reverberate with the sound of bomb blasts, shaken by one explosion after another.

The shutters drop. Pedestrians, rickshaw-pullers, street-dogs, begin to run. Inside a jhopri—hut—near the railway lines, Hamid and Nelo look at each other.

Nelo says, The police will start firing.

Which side is the sound coming from?

Near the cinema hall.

Then they won't fire.

Why?

It's just Germany's gang.

Oh!

In reality, this town has many gangs, many divisions. A small town. But since it is near the border, since there is an abundant supply of essential commodities like smuggled guns, brassieres, drugs, 'Monaco' brand cassette-players, adulterated medicines, blue films in 'Jawan' video-cassettes (foreign goods), this small town generates brisk business; trade flourishes.

Besides, the business of smuggling of cows, goats, rice and clothes from one side of the border to another, that too is no less profitable.

It's because of all this that the *controllers* don't want to relinquish their hold on this town. They are also the rulers. Germany, Sachcha, Baba, Bota, Paolan—these are the select few worthy citizens known to the rest of the town's residents as the *controllers*.

They believe in 'freedom', in 'struggle'. Let the black-marketeers do what they want. They must be given the 'freedom' to carry on with business as usual. The *controllers* collect paybacks from them on a regular basis.

Just as this fundamental 'freedom' is ensured, so too the 'struggle' to take over parts of the town, to lay claim to new avenues of trade, must be allowed to continue unimpeded. The five *controllers* struggle. And five more of the *pablic*[1] get killed. Support from the local police station is not to be taken for granted since that is dependent on various other factors. One of the determining factors is the will of the two political parties; which *controller* is currently the champion of which party? Since all five of them provide paybacks to the thana, the police do not really believe in controlling the *controllers*.

A lot had been written about this, a lot of muck had been raked up, but to no avail. The only good that came out of it once was when the magistrate and the police superintendent were both transferred out of the area soon after the arrest of a *mastaan*.

The Thana-babu is unperturbed. He is a rare Thana-babu indeed, one who, despite being repeatedly gheraoed by the angry *pablic*, just sits there unconcerned, doesn't turn a hair.

The reason: 'Jyotisharnab'[2] Bhola-babu. The thana building and the lock-up collapsed four times—each time within three to five months of its renewed construction—yet the same contractor, protégé to a certain political leader, kept getting the job. The fifth time, just before resuming work, the contractor's patron (the certain political leader) forgot his advanced years and duodenal ulcer, gorged on huge helpings of hilsas from the Ganga and tiger prawns from the saltwater marshes (the dishes prepared with generous portions of chillies, both whole and ground to a paste), all at the contractor's expense, and then died of a duodenal disorder in the sweltering heat of a Jaishtha[3] afternoon.

His death left in the lurch not only his wife, sons, daughters, sons-in-law, daughters-in-law, brothers-in-law (on his side of the family), more brothers-in-law (on the wife's side of the family), hundreds of relatives, both near and distant but many others too who found themselves suddenly rudderless.

Those who had set sail, secure with him at the helm, now found themselves abandoned in mid-ocean. With no sight of land. Such as his protégé, the contractor. What would he do now, without his mentor? The new leader belonged to a rival faction in the party, nursed a grouse against him.

The contractor believed in revolution, and in Bhola-babu. Bhola-babu lent a compassionate ear to his tales of woes. Then he said, Look here! Then, your Jupiter was in the ascendant. Your patron too was alive. You could do as you pleased. But now . . .

I'll die!

No, Nityahari, you won't. You got the contract four times, for the same building. You were paid in full each time. Built yourself five houses, bought four Matador cars. You won't die.

But I couldn't make it to the finals!

You could have. Why did you stuff that dyspeptic old bag full of hilsas and prawns, that too on a hot summer afternoon? If you'd fed him with thankuni[4]-leaf shukto[5] and magur[6] curry instead, you'd have been able to build the thana ten times over.

What now?

Your stars are unfavourable. Hear me? I'll take care of that. But this time the job must be honestly done. Convince yourself that you're working for the public. You want to line your pockets, I know. But don't forget where you come from. The land of Bagha Jatin, Ashananda Dhenki,[7] Gobinda Pal (the recently-deceased leader). All sons of this district. Don't forget . . .

I won't.

This time I'll prepare the horoscope of the thana. Work must begin bang on time, right at the auspicious moment. If you goof this one up, that's the end of you in *town*.

Work began as per Bhola-babu's instructions. For the first time, the best bricks. The best sand, the best cement, genuine raw materials were used. A long horoscope of the thana was prepared. Reading it through, Thana-babu said, I get whatever you've written about the newborn, but what's this *munchati-jeebanancha-gangajaley*[8] bit.

Why?

How can the thana be wiped out this way? Submerged in the Ganges? The river's 16 miles off to the west.

Don't speak like a non-believer! thundered Jyotisharnab, the great astrologer. This new thana will last two hundred years. In that time the river will have shifted to this side, did you know that? Mother Ganga has so long been flowing westward. The future will see her flowing eastward. Didn't you see in 1978 how the thana was submerged in the floodwaters of the Ganga? It was not written that it should be destroyed then, hence it has survived.

But now . . .

Now Jupiter will remain in the ascendant.

That horoscope lies safe in the custody of the Thana-babu, carefully preserved like the *time capsule*. Thus, whether it be the public, the newspapers or the magistrate, the Thana-babu remains unperturbed, unafraid.

At present, inexplicably enough, the thana is lending its support to the *controller* Germany. When the newspapers in Calcutta report, 'No Peace in this Town!', 'Town in the Grip of Gangsters', Thanababu is hurt by the words.

He wants peace too. It's only those five *mastaans* who harass the public so.

Selling a house? Where's our share?

Buying a house? Where's our share?

Selling land? Where's our share?

Buying land? Where's our share?

Selling goods in the market? Where's our share?

A fixed commission from every shopkeeper every day.

A few bombs your way should you write about us in the local dailies.

Marrying off your daughter? Where's our share?

Collecting your pension money? Where's our share?

Organized a protest against *bulu philms*[9] being shown in *town*? Get bombed.

Beaten up Ryanda for raping your sister? Eat bullets.

Not one but if four hundred '20-point programmes'[10] are run by only five people, how can there be any hope of peace in the life of the public? The five hundredth birth anniversary of the divine 'P'em-er Thakur'[11] and still no peace prevails in this district!

All because of those five who rule the land.

Thana-babu understands the plight of the *pablic*. Thus, he is trying his utmost to see to it that the five are reduced to one. He himself does not have the power to unite them. So Thana-babu's efforts are directed by either human or divine agency.

To make sure that Germany rules alone.

Let Germany snuff out Sachcha, Baba, Bota, Paolan. Then Thana-babu will personally announce that some 'anti-socials' or 'extremists' have been removed. (Those were Thana-babu's Orders.)

Oh for that auspicious day, to see Germany reigning supreme. Finally, some peace for the *pablic*. Only one target, how can five people each want a share?

But no one understands his logic. Not even Malati, an elderly prostitute in the *line*.

Having served in the *line* for many years, Malati has now taken to serving the people. More specifically, serving each customer who walks through her doors. This girl's okay. Not that one. She's infected. And other such pearls of wisdom. But Thana-babu fails to convince even Malati of his strategy for a peaceful *town*.

Malati asks him, Why? Why let only Germany rule, and why get rid of the rest? Why not let them all rot in hell? And I don't understand all that talk of one portion shared between five people. If you're so concerned about the *pablic*, then why burden them with even one of those five? Let everyone live their own lives.

You don't understand.

I understand perfectly well. Pona-babu sold his land, and those five grabbed the commission. It's unfair. Wrong. Besides, do your words hold true for everyone?

Why?

This *line*'s no good any more. Illegal trade's sprouting up everywhere. Never mind that. Doesn't a whore share her one piece with not only five but countless more?

Thana-babu says, How do I explain! She sells the same thing five times, and gets paid each time. But here, the *pablic* has to cough up money five times over for the same thing.

Oh!

Never read Economics, did you!

Read *Kamikhheytantra*,[12] *Master–Chhatri Katha*, *Grihasth-er Totka*, *Kamini Kaaman Daagey*[13] . . . isn't that enough!

Oh yes, quite enough!

Look here! I'm not one of your upstart whores. My family's been in the *line* for generations. I'm a woman of honour. No matter what you say, I don't think it's a good idea to knock off the others for Germany's sake. Germany's a coward. Useless without his gang. Don't rely on him. I care about the thana, depend on it, so I'm trying to knock some sense into you.

Malati's real income these days comes from hooch, receiving and distributing. She passes on information to the thana as and when necessary. Despite this, Thana-babu cannot accept Malati's orders to 'let them all rot in hell'. He is a slave to his Orders. His Orders are, '*Up, up Germany. Give him a political colour.*'

But what *colour* can he paint him? No one wants Germany. Orders are easily issued, but not so easy to execute.

Malati says, I can't stand Germany, babu. Said so to his face.

Why?

Because of that Phulbanu . . . Wasn't Hamid's own child but he got her off the streets, looked after her. He'd practice throwing daggers, she'd stand there, watching. Before you know it she's thirteen. She's pretty. So many times I'd said to Hamid, She's not safe in this hellish *town*. Give her to me. I'll fix her with a *bandha-babu*, a regular. She'll be safe, you'll get your money. But would Hamid listen? Kept saying, She's my *jaan*.[14] I'll arrange her shaadi[15] . . . Then Germany grabbed her . . .

It had been to the thana that Hamid had come running, carrying the body of Phulbanu, the little girl who'd been raped and then murdered. Despite knowing that Germany was the culprit, Thana-babu arrested a rickshaw-puller instead and set him up for trial. There has still been no trial. He is still a prisoner.

Hamid went away, where? Then again, he's returned a while back, a boy called Nelo with him.

Not just once! So many little girls . . .

Forget it!

It is true that Germany is a coward. His clout, stemming entirely from the thana's support. Why can't he just wipe out Sachcha, Baba, Bota and Paolan? The thana's behind him, after all.

No, no! Their gang members will carve me up.

Even with me on your side?

They'll skip off across the *bodar*.[16] Then?

No, Thana-babu is finding it difficult to *up* Germany. He is trying his best. But he just cannot find a suitable colour from the political paintbox to paint Germany with.

Which colour to choose? Which shade to white-wash with?

The *town*'s hardly got enough colours either. The prevailing red has grown murky, a mix of many colours. The Opposition colours too have curdled into a strange shade, what with every other colour being stirred into its own. That leaves him with just red, bright red.

But Thana-babu's guts aren't tough enough for that. Although every killing, every *action*—of inter-gang warfare, of area-occupation struggle—between Germany, Baba, Bota, Sachcha and Paolan (different from Paloan, operating across the border), is uniformly passed off by Thana-babu in his report as 'inter-party clashes among anti-social extremists'.

And the Calcutta journalists rip his report to shreds, lay bare the actual picture.

The situation's intolerable, intolerable!

Not for Thana-babu. But for the *pablic*.

But the most distressing news for the thana is the formation of a citizens' committee in the town, one that has united the people despite their individual political leanings and party affiliations.

The death—by mass lynching—sentence passed on Ryanda and Bota is no less distressing.

Something similar happened just a few days ago.

When two of Germany's followers, Gola and Kaan (Thana-babu fails to understand why he is called Kaan, because one of his *kaans*, or ears, is missing) tried in retaliation to bomb the house of Akhil-babu, the elderly leader of the citizens' committee, they were (i) caught by the *pablic*, (ii) thrashed to within an inch of their lives, (iii) a sackful of fresh bombs was dumped into the tank and destroyed (what a waste!), and (iv) the followers of all the political parties along with the common people deposited the two of them at the thana. And then left, with a warning in Thana-babu's direction. Let them out and it'll be your turn next.

Jyotisharnab, the great astrologer, is also not in town. Away at Amarnath, then a stop at Hardwar, and then back home. At his devotees' expense. Many contractors have become his devotees, now. He's careful, however, never to stuff himself full of rich food at their expense. Travels on his pilgrimages in air-conditioned First Class compartments. Also travels frequently to New Delhi—the supreme pilgrimage spot. Has established his son there. Visits him now and then, keeps an eye on how he's faring. Astrologers are currently very much in demand in New Delhi, both among the ruling and the Opposition parties. Jyotisharnab predicts, Get a hundred or so Bengali astrologers and that's it. Work's done. But astrologers of that state are paid no attention, yet another instance of the 'Centre's conspiracy against the State'.

He has a second son. Supplies contracted labour. Doesn't know astrology.

There is thus no one here now to tell Thana-babu how long the rapidly increasing influence of the citizens' committee will last.

Listening to the successive explosions issuing from the direction of the cinema hall tonight, Thana-babu can tell that it is Germany's *action*. [17]

But against whom? Who lives there?

The news arrives the next morning. But not at the thana.

A huge procession had been organized, carrying the bodies of a peanut-vendor and two rickshaw-pullers who were killed last night for taking part in a peace campaign. The slogans were extremely upsetting.

Bring down anti-social terrorism, bring it down!

Notorious gangsters Germany, Baba, Sachcha and Paolan—arrest them, arrest them!

Who threw the bombs yesterday?

Taja, Chhyanda and Keshtokali!

Who's their leader?

Police's goonda Germany!

Bring down the rule of terror, bring it down!

Bring down the thana inspector, bring him down!

Compensation to the families of the dead! Compensation to the families of Amar Das, Dilip Das and Shahjahan!

The protest march circles the small town a few times. Then congregates in front of the thana where the bodies are laid down and a meeting is held. Thana-babu is petrified. Should he hurl tear gas or fire bullets? At the meeting, which is being addressed by Akhil-babu and Gopen-babu of the ruling party, Subodh-babu and Chandra-babu of the Opposition, two college principals, five headmasters–headmistresses and three doctors?

Thana-babu steps outside. No choice but to yield to circumstance.

Akhil-babu is middle-aged, dyspeptic, but still respected as an honest man. Extremely short of temper.

He snaps, Step forward.

Thana-babu steps forward.

We'll take a *deputation* to Krishnanagar. Organize a press conference in Calcutta.

Of course you will.

You must immediately arrest Taja, Chhyanda and Keshtokali. Immediately.

They threw the bombs?

No, I did!

Gopen-babu speaks up, I've seen them. I was in the neighbourhood, visiting my daughter. I saw them, looked through the window-slats.

Rajat the youth leader says, If the thana doesn't take *action*, the people of this town will.

Akhil-babu adds, Instead of a death every other day, let's wipe them out once and for all. Lay down our lives.

Chandra-babu says, We've sent a written *report* to Calcutta, understand?

Subodh-babu is a trader, a veteran theatre actor as well. He used to act once upon a time, played Chanakya, Durgadas, Chandrashekhar, many other roles. Even now when he speaks, it's as though he is struggling to remember the lines. Pauses, often. His voice, loud, strident.

He says, We, ten *leading* citizens of this town, and ninety other well-known names are submitting to you a signed memorandum demanding their arrest. Copies have been sent to *Writers'*[18] and the newspapers. We want immediate *action*.

Ultimately, Thana-babu has no choice but to embark on a campaign of his own. Keshtokali has disappeared (discovered the next day, stuffed under a clump of yam shrubs. In all probability, the bomb had exploded while still clutched in his hand). Taja and Chhyanda (Ryanda's brother) do not resist arrest. The *tempo*'s not good, times are bad. It's safer inside the lock-up. They both bid farewell to Germany. We're copping out, *guru*![19] Even Paolan gives his men better *p'otection*.[20]

Public pressure forces the police to conduct further raids. Some are dead, some are rushing to cross the border, some are nabbed. Baba, Sachcha and Paolan have probably escaped to Calcutta on the night bus or truck.

Akhil-babu says, Beat them up. Make them spill the beans, who's hiding where.

Germany smoulders helplessly in rage and humiliation. Akhil-babu must be removed. He's the one egging on the rest of the committee.

Meanwhile, the citizens' committee, successful in moving the police to act, walk through the town, their loudspeakers issuing a call for an emergency meeting. Tomorrow is Sunday. We are meeting at

ten in the morning. Come to Subhash Park. Come
one, come all. Nothing to fear. Gauribari has shown
us the way. Anantapur will not lag behind.[21]

Germany is grim. His toadies have gone underground. He is a marked man. It will be difficult
for him to enter Akhil-babu's house. Besides, the
committee has also formed vigilant squads. They pa-
trol the streets at night.

Malati says, There's no use worrying.

Let's see.

Malati's hooch supplier, Pakhi, was once an *ac-
tion-master* in Lalgola. But alas, these days, God looks
after good folks no more! Once, after a dacoity near
the border, drunk on vast quantities of booze, he
climbed atop an abandoned rail wagon, stretched
out his arms, shouting, I can fly! I can fly! and then
leapt into the air.

The result was a hundred different hassles all at
once. Arrested as a criminal and simultaneously admitted into hospital with broken arms and legs. In
the hospital, his right hand was amputated, his right
leg stayed crippled.

Pakhi had been an expert knifer. Now he is handicapped, disabled. He moans continually, If only I could use my arm today . . .

He tells Germany, This is not a job for bombs or rifles. It's a knife-job. Just a *throw* of the knife, that's all. If I still had that right arm . . .

An annoyed Malati says, Shut up. Delivered the goods, got your money, now get lost. The *van* won't wait for you, I hope you know that.

He leaves. Malati and Germany. Malati offers Germany his commission. He waves it aside.

No need.

You won't take it now?

I won't take it at all, this time.

Why?

I've got a job for you.

What job?

Do you know where Hamid stays?

I know.

He'll have to come, once.

Hamid?

Yes, I'll talk to him.

Talk . . . to him . . . ?

Tell him that I'm quitting *town*. I want to give him . . . give him some money.

Malati, her head bent low as she slices betel-nuts. Why should he come? He's scared of you.

That's why he'll come. If he wants to stay in *town* . . .

Where should he come?

Why, my place?

He won't have the guts.

But I'm alone now.

Even then.

Then, behind the lumber-stack.

Which one?

In the cremation ground.

Okay.

Go now.

I'll go tomorrow. I'm night-blind, didn't you know?

Tomorrow night, at nine.

Malati says she'll go.

He comes to the market every morning.

I'll go, I've just said so.

Germany leaves, brandishing his revolver. Malati thinks, Has Germany forgotten about Phulbanu? Why is he looking for Hamid? Does he want to use him to . . . Akhil-babu . . . No! Malati won't think. What good can thinking do?

Malati's night-blindness or lack thereof depends purely upon her instincts of self-preservation. If she must meet Hamid, it's best done now. In the daytime, there'll be people, she'll be spotted. There'll be witnesses. If Akhil-babu is . . . will Malati be able to escape, then?

She grabs a torch, steps out.

The streets are deserted. A few cops. Malati's is a familiar face. Only she can walk the streets at this hour. The *pablic* know the faces of her customers. And her. Just an old hooch-dealing whore. The thana and the *mastaans* get *cuts,* commissions. The rickshaw-pullers have recently started saying, Mashi, don't give them anything.

Let others stop. Then I will too.

Why don't you lead the way?

No mister! The thana-and-*mastaans*, like fish-and-curry. These arrests're just for show. If I knew that the *town* was truly cleansed . . .

His abortive flight and its various fallouts later, Pakhi has now turned to philosophy. He has advised Malati before leaving, See everything, do nothing. Don't be swept off your feet. The *Kaliyugamahatma* tells us that *mastaans* are essential in this day and age. They who wipe out one bunch of gangsters are the ones who install another. You vote, send your representative. If he dies, does his seat stay empty? When the wife dies, the husband marries; when the husband dies, the wife marries. If there's no *mastaan*, if there's no *controller*, who will look after all this? The thana will go into mourning!

Malati has thus become the repository of the *town*'s news. News that will result in another corpse is not conveyed to the thana. After all, she's not an upstart whore! One in a long tradition of whores. A woman of honour. Malati's heard how her grand-mother had once sheltered *swadeshi*-babus[22] on the run and at the same time, flirted with the darogas who were their pursuers.

Malati will inform Hamid, Hamid will obey Germany's orders, she can see it all so clearly. Phul-banu! What of one Phulbanu, dead or alive, Hamid! She's dead, but you're still alive! Phulbanus die, Ger-manys live on.

Gravel along the railway tracks, the shrubs reeking of shit. Malati enters Hamid's jhopri.

Hamid listens, listens to everything. Nelo's asleep. Malati does not explain the job. Hamid just keeps nodding his head.

Go back, mashi. I'll go tomorrow.

Go. You know . . .

I know.

Malati leaves. Hamid sits there. How his pulse races, how his blood surges in excitement!

Thana-babu has said, on the sly, Get Germany's *p'otection*. Or I'll drive you out of *town* under the Vagrancy Act.

Yes, babu.

Forget the past.

Yes, babu.

Good you've brought along a boy now. A boy, eh? No one will notice him.

Yes, babu.

What else can you do? The likes of you, earning a bit or two, all have to seek *p'otection*. Be it the snake-charmer, or the monkey-man. Times are bad.

Hamid remembers it all. Everything is Germany's. When will Germany, like that genie of Baghdad, reach up to the skies and extort *p'otection* money from the sun, moon and stars? When will he burrow into the earth and ask the fields of grain for *p'otection* money? Will no one ever be able to resist him?

The next day there is a mass rally at Subhash Park. Among the speakers, it is Akhil-babu who snarls the most. Subodh-babu and a headmaster speak in softer tones. They all say the same thing. The police and the administration have failed to suppress the terror of the *mastaans*. Appeals, petitions, deputations, thana-gheraos, all in vain. See, our citizens' committee. Irrespective of party affiliations, we are all united. It's our problem. We'll have to solve it.

Yesterday's events have been reported faithfully if not entirely in most of the newspapers. Our movement shall continue as long the *mastaan*-raj reigns.

Rajat, Panu, Chanchal, Shanto, Somesh (*targets* now, due to sudden cracks appearing in their political loyalties) also add their bits. We must be brave. You, the people, you are the citizens' committee. If those whose lives are endangered do not step forward . . .

The air thick with slogans, shouted over and over again.

No more extorting from the poor!

No more molesting women!

For all killings–clashes–conflicts over the last two years, we want an independent inquiry, we want justice!

Notorious goondas Germany, Baba, Sachcha and Paolan—we want them arrested, we want them tried!

The thana's role to be investigated! Suitable steps taken against it!

The struggle of the citizens' committee continues today, continues tomorrow!

Germany hears it all. It's a small town. A loudspeaker blares even at the mouth of his lane. No sounds from the cinema hall either. There's a two-day strike in protest of day-before-yesterday's bomb blasts. Germany lies in bed, listens. Go on, keep going. I'll begin with Akhil-babu. Once he's bumped off (a ruling party man) the other old bastards will lose their nerve. A bit of mayhem in town. Then my chamchas[23] will return. This time Germany'll bring Kamal from Siliguri. Kamal will use his *sten* to polish off Paolan and the others, then disappear.

He'll take money! So what! Even Hamid will have to be given money. It would have been good if I could use Hamid always.

Paolan himself and his chamchas are experts with the *chaku*, the knife. Germany has no such talent in his gang. If Hamid stayed with him, he could at least be trained. You're my man, Hamid!

Germany has been placed on the earth solely to think of himself. He does not think of others. Phulbanu had been just a little girl, just like many others. Twelve to thirteen, young, unmarked and whole. So hard to find a body, fleshy, yet chaste! Malati has promised him one if she ever finds it.

Such pleasure in the rape, and such pleasure in the kill. Germany will never be able to explain the ecstasy of it all.

The cremation ground. The lumber-stack. Behind the lumber-stack, the paddy-field. This is Germany's *elaka*, his territory. He is safe.

Germany leans against the banyan tree.

Hamid is silent.

No one will suspect you. You can enter the neighbourhood. The old man sits on the porch every day.

Police?

I'll manage a *load-shedding*.[24]

Police?

I'll post bail.

Oh!

You used to fling daggers. And knives?

I use knives now. It's all the same, depends on the *throw* . . .

Finish the job. Get paid.

Five hundred now. Five hundred after.

Hamid stares at him. Germany has no regrets about Phul-*jaan*. No fear about summoning Hamid. He's Germany. His will be done.

Will you do it?

Of course.

Here's the money.

Give me money, give me money, Germany!

Some day you'll be alone, Hamid will be waiting, watching. It is with this hope that Hamid has returned to *town*. The citizens' committee has given him that chance.

Just Akhil-babu?

For the moment. Later, there's Subodh-babu . . . Rajat . . .

The money!

Here.

Germany takes a step forward, Hamid suddenly moves backward.

What was that, slithering, that way? Quick, shine your torch.

Germany brings out his torch. Hamid moves back a little further. A professional knifer requires a measured distance.

Germany-babu!

Germany looks up.

A flash in the darkness. The unerring point of the long knife pierces Germany's throat, pins him to the tree. The second knife is aimed at the heart. The torch drops to the ground. Germany-babu! For this one moment I've been throwing knives for so long, shown off my skill, practised *spring-knives* on the board, for so long.

Hamid runs home.

Once in *town*, he slows down. Walks normally. He goes to his jhopri.

Nelo's dozing, the rice cooked.

Hamid says, Let's go, Nelo.

Where, ustad?

Just come with me.

The rice?

The dogs'll eat it. Fold the board.

Hamid and Nelo start walking along the highway. Reach the next stop. Not for Calcutta. Board a truck for Dalkhola. Get off at Siliguri. Head towards North Bengal. Or Malda, then Bangladesh.

The truck will stop. People have been leaving Anantapur, disappearing for a while. The trucks know. The trucks stop.

Hamid gets on the truck. Looks up at the sky. No, the sky today is the real sky. Not blotted out by some genie's head. Nelo doses. Hamid holds him in his arms. We'll eat somewhere on the way, Nelo. Then lose ourselves in the sea of humanity.

He tells Nelo, You'll have to learn the game.

Nelo sleeps.

The next morning the *town* reels, as though struck by lightning. Germany killed in his own territory, his money untouched! A *spring-knife* job. How they crowd before the thana to have a look at the body! Malati comes too, expresses shock before the others, asks, Who killed him?

Thana-babu's head, struck by *load-shedding*. Darkness. Paolan and the others will hear the news, come back to *town*. The *chaku* was their speciality. Nab them? But what are the Orders, his Orders?

Whom to arrest? What colour to choose, what colour to paint them with?

Crackers and fireworks go off in town, celebrations, crowds thronging the streets.

The truck carries Germany to the morgue.

Thana-babu waits for Orders. Baba, Paolan, Sachcha, who will fill the gap?

Whom to arrest? The poor are leaving the town every day, day after day.

Thana-babu waits, keeps waiting for Orders.

Malati gives him a bottle of good hooch today. Must be sad. Here, have a drink.

Who did it, Malati?

Don't know. But people're saying you've got it done, because of the citizens' committee. Now you're playing dumb.

Thana-babu sits, *load-shedding* in his head. Only the Orders will turn the lights back on.

Then?

Malati?

Malati says, tenderly, Have a drink.

Thana-babu has a drink. The *pablic* thinks he's done it? Because of the citizens' committee?

Transfer? Punishment posting? The town is

rejoicing at the end of the *mastaan*-raj. The end of the *mastaan*-raj? Thana-babu bursts into tears.

The end of his present, his future, dark. There will be no forgiveness. He has failed to save Germany.

Malati says, Dry your tears. Have a drink.

III

Body

1

The girl drives a silver Fiat, arrives at the Gariahat[1] crossing late in the evening. Parks the car at the *boulevard*. Stands on the left footpath. A black car drives up, on the other side, in front of the market. A young boy at the wheel. He does not get out. His hair, even at this age, has turned grey. He usually wears white. He sits in the car. He watches the girl.

Sometimes the girl walks over. Speaks to the boy. Brings out a handkerchief, wipes the nape of her neck. Then comes back to her car, drives away. On the other side, the black car too, slowly, leaves.

Sometimes the girl doesn't speak to anyone.

And the black car doesn't wait, drives off swiftly.

2

Sometimes, in the evening, the girl drives her silver Fiat to Ballygunge, in front of that tea-shop. The young boy steps out of the black car. Both of them enter the tea-shop. They don't speak to each other. Sometimes the girl talks to another boy. This young man leaves, then. Although only after the girl has brought out her handkerchief, wiped her neck. Most of the time the girl doesn't speak to anyone. The young boy however speaks to the shop-owner, chats. The young boy never forgets to wear white.

3

Sometimes, in the afternoon, the girl drives her silver Fiat to *patuapara*, the potters' colony,[2] in front of that house. A black car arrives, parks on the other side, hugging the edge of the footpath. A young boy at the wheel . . .

There is no sign of the girl's silver car in the morning. She sleeps late into the day. Her night begins later, deep into the night—when street-dogs sleep, when the cats curl up on the cornices. When the moonlight and neonlight seek rest, when only the few statues remain standing in the streets, when the city is asleep. Except perhaps the cockroaches, the rats. In the dockyards, this is when the rats hunt sleeping sailors, lolling beggars, cautiously nibble at their feet, the flesh at their heels, then scurry off into the darkness. Human flesh is a great favourite. Legend has it that once upon a time even Bimbisara's[3] wife was fond of human flesh and then . . .

The girl returns to her flat by eight. Straight to the bathroom. For a *steam-bath*. A must. Because very soon he will come to her who is by name and nature Nripati, 'The Emperor'. At one time he donated a lot of his ancestral property in a spirit of 'come-one-come-all, take-one-take-all' largesse. Today, he belongs to 'everyone', but just like an orthodox Hindu widow won't touch masoor dal and turmeric,[4] he too won't touch a girl if her skin's not clean. Frantically running from one end of Bengal to the other, meetings, lectures, efforts to revive this nation from its ignominious death-like stupor, he is now almost 60. Yet, like his father (a French jockey), he is still a towering hulk of a man. Even he never forgets his *steam-baths*. At his age, he has maintained up to 15 separate flats in Calcutta for 15 separate girls, at one time or another. He is the one who fits up each flat with its own *steam-bath*. Yelling on behalf of the 'Common Man!' is one thing but, after all, how 'common' can Nripati allow himself to be? With his French blood and his Bengali identity?

Installs a *steam-bath* in every flat, and approaches Mr M for girls. M's full name cannot be revealed but surely it is evident that M is an operator. His operations mathematically accurate, axiomatic, like the signs of the Zodiac. If Nripati needs a mistress, he will have to go to M, to operators like him. Besides, Nripati nurses an intense fascination for ugly faces with beautiful bodies. Such girls are freely available these days from the lower classes. This girl's speciality, of course, is different. Her parents belonged to some tribal community. Both, arrested after several murders. Both, hanged. The little girl grew up as a ward of the state. Went to school, joined college. It is best to make no mention of her face. Her face, hewn out of some ancient, craggy rock. Her expression, usually inscrutable. But who cares about the face, it's her body, her body, like the goddess of a pre-historic people. Black, primeval, brutal, frightening.

And her courage. And her unshakeable loyalty. And the other thing that attracted M was her seeming disregard for all ethics and morality.

The girl takes a bath. Wears pretty clothes. Comes out of her room. A knock at her door. That young boy. Two knocks. M. Sometimes the girl gets an envelope from M. She puts it away in her steel *almirah*.

Then they leave. Then Nripati arrives. Sometimes he carries on a question-and-answer session with her, thus. It is the girl who asks the questions. Of late she has begun to doubt.

This using me to trap them . . .

You know how they are.

Why kill them?

Best that way.

If they ever come to know . . . ?

They'll chop you to bits.

Me? The girl falls silent. Thinks.

Nripati asks, That one . . . your . . . ? No news of him?

No.

Still love him?

The girl doesn't reply. Looks at Nripati with slightly startled eyes. Why do you help us? Because M says so?

Yes.

Because the girl is grateful to M. Extremely grateful. She is captive in M's clutches, powerless. She'd steal from one shop to the other until they caught her, issued a warning. Then she'd befriend strangers in sleazy bars. Pretend to help them, filch their wallets. Got arrested one evening helping a professor for real. She'd been so stunned to find him there. He was the one who'd invite students home, spend time talking, explaining. The same house where she'd go just for a closer look at Anupam. Just to be in the same room. The others would talk, discuss, read books and magazines. The girl would only look at Anupam. Then, one day, Anupam stopped coming. Then, one day, Anupam turned into a VIP. The girl had gone to him then, offered herself. Anupam hadn't been fair to her that day but he had certainly been astonished by the girl's *logic*.

The girl wants Anupam. In this world, if you want anything, you have to give something in exchange. The girl wants to give herself, since she has nothing else, nothing special. Anupam, of course, vanished from her life, left without a trace, left without a word. The girl does not remember those days in her life; what did she do, where did she go? Wandering the streets of Calcutta, frantic, demented. Sometimes she'd feel as if, finally, Anupam had been forgotten, finally, the ache was gone. But the moment she woke up, opened her eyes, she'd know that the ache still throbbed, intact. She'd begun visiting other places, meeting other people.

Enough of that. When she spotted the professor in the bar, her first thought had been about Anupam. She'd taken the professor by the hand, wanting to take him home. She'd picked up his wallet from the floor, tried to return it, when he began to yell, Thief! Thief!

Thus, back to the thana–police–OC—wading through the pale cream-coloured sheets of paper, thumbing through the forms printed in fading ink, crammed with A-B-Cs and other shapes. M said, Ketaki, you!

Just like a kitten noses its way back home, just like a duckling takes to the water, M is quite amazed by this girl who too seems to possess a similar *homing instinct* in making her way back to the cops. M tried to change her ways for the better, true, but then she was spotted by Nripati. The same Nripati who has freely given his all to the masses, who has kept only this for himself, squeezed between his committees and his speeches, this secret life of flats–girls–*steam-baths*.

When Nripati asks her, Why do you do this?, the girl stares at him for a while. When he persists with, Because M says so?, she nods in agreement.

Much later, she asks, And why do you? Because you're afraid of them? Your gang . . . and M's gang . . . couldn't you . . . ?

Nripati slaps her, hits her face with the palm of his left hand. A blunt smacking sound. Blood trickles down her chin. The sight of her own blood, even now, can drive the girl crazy. This is an *instinct* that is part of that very blood. She has never seen her parents but they too had grabbed their scythes in self-defence, only after they had been hit, only after their blood, this blood, was spilt.

The girl wipes away the blood. Then says, That son of yours. The one who plays the guitar. Did you know he came here, the other day? Asking for a glass of water. As if there's nowhere else in the city.

Nripati pulls her to himself with his right hand. In his left hand, now, a glass. Equally adept with both his hands, hence Nripati is also revered as 'Sabyasachi'.[5]

That night, almost at daybreak, Anupam came to the girl. Not to her in particular, any shelter would do. Any shelter, anywhere to hide, for a while.

Tui? You? Anupam's hand slipped automatically into his pocket. Self-preservation. Instinct. That old impulse, yet his wrist devoid of strength.

The girl and Anupam stand there, staring at each other, for a few moments. The girl's clothes, the furniture, the glasses strewn everywhere, Nripati's favourite album of dirty pictures (lying open on the carpet), yet Anupam says nothing. Just asks, Are you alone? This time, the more formal *tumi*.

Yes.

Can you keep me here? Until tomorrow.

I can. Tomorrow, tomorrow, I'll reach you wherever you want to go. You're on the run, escaping, aren't you? I have a car.

She led Anupam into her bedroom. Asked him to lock the door, from within. She sat outside. Stayed there, sitting. Then, at one time, fell asleep. It was the first time she forgot that she had somewhere to go in her silver Fiat. The afternoon rolled by.

Then, Atanu came. Atanu, M, other people, many other people. The sound of boots marching up the stairs.

All Anupam asked was, How much will you get?

What do you think the girl did? That night, Nripati, M, all in her flat, a mad frenzy of celebration. She could have shot them. She could have stirred poison in their drinks. But she did nothing like that.

She locked the bathroom door. Then, a thud. Voices screaming, downstairs. Nripati and M peeped out from the eighth-floor window, looked down. A body, strange, broken, lying on the footpath. For hundreds of pairs of eyes to see, their two faces, side by side, remain frozen in the square of the window-pane, trapped, in the lens of the window's camera.

IV

Killer

1

HOW OLD IS AKHIL, what does he do, why was he in
Coochbehar, why is he returning to Calcutta, why
isn't he carrying any luggage—no matter how hard
he tried to evade answering each of these questions,
the woman, for some reason, was gripped with a
tremendous curiosity about him. An elderly woman,
probably as old as his mother. She would have been

mortified if she ever found out that every answer Akhil had given her had been a lie.

To begin with, Akhil's name is not Akhil. He will respond sure enough if you call out 'Sona', a name after all a habit that runs in your blood. It is only in the foreign thrillers that international spies arrive in three different continents, fly into three different capitals, their passports bearing a new name each time. And a few glasses of expensive liquor on the flight. Just as they never get drunk on alcohol, just as they never get killed by the enemy's assassins, so too they never fail to remember, to respond, to their ever-changing names.

Akhil hasn't read any foreign thrillers.

Thus it had taken him a lot of time to get used to his new name. Even now, a suddenly shouted 'Sona' on the streets will make him swing around in response.

He is twenty-six years old. Although, because of the lines on his face, his greying hair, because of the mesh of wrinkles that criss-cross at the corner of his eyes, like marks left on the mud by the feet of little birds, because of his vacant stony gaze, because he never smiles, he looks old, middle-aged. He'd told the woman that he was forty. She'd said she thought he was older.

I'm a businessman, he'd said. He is actually a professional killer. Killed thirty-one young boys in two years. If he hadn't killed the first time, he'd have been killed himself. He'd been given nothing for the job, the first time. But it would be wrong to say that he got nothing out of it, nothing at all. No event or action goes unrewarded in this world. Perhaps there are no material gains in exchange but the experience, the emotions it arouses, those are gains too.

He discovered himself after that first killing. Discovered he was a killer, that was his true identity. This discovery was an important event, at least for him. Since then . . .

He was paid for the other thirty. Or else he wouldn't have agreed. And that's the money that's seeing him through, all this time. Just that last occasion when he failed. 'Failed' but didn't leave the job unfinished. But failed nonetheless because he had not anticipated that Sajad Mandal the peasant, mere skin and bone, could have the strength to hurl that tin mug at his eyes, bludgeon him over and over again with that brick in such ferocious protest.

And his mind, strange creature that it was, its confidence unshaken only as long as his jobs went off smoothly. But when he came back after finishing the job, after the unexpected attack by Sajad Mandal, Anupam Mitra, exhaling expensive cigar smoke, had said, You're losing *form*. Better stay *off* now.

Even then he never realized that Anupam-da was inserting a *semi-colon* in his *career*. Soon after that, at least two jobs in his territory, done by others. A great insult. Causing him to come to blows with Khoka and Taju. But they had given him a terrific beating. They had been taught by the right sources, how to beat a man without leaving any marks whatsoever. Sona hadn't known that severe blows to the tendons at the elbow could leave both arms disabled for a long time. One could say that they beat him like a cur. He wasn't possessed of their *training*, of Khoka and Taju's higher education.

He'd grown frightened, since then. Everything was getting confused, his *career*, in peril. His livelihood, threatened. The enemy was incredibly powerful. He hadn't realized how much. But Anupam-da, exhaling expensive cigar smoke, had said, A *take-over* by the *professionals* is on. Better stay *off* now.

Professional? The word makes him angry, sad too. Killing is a recognized *profession*. You kill, because you have to. You are not to involve any personal emotions. You will not regard your victim as a boy–teenager–young man. You will not think about his mind or his heart, his parents, his lover, the mark of a childhood vaccination on his arm, his talent for writing poetry, the *dot-pen*[1] in his pocket, that is, you will not think about anything that identifies him as a human being. For you, he is nothing more than a *case*. You will not make his death a prolonged, time-consuming affair. Unlike Khoka and Taju, you do not use iron rods, knives, bricks, all at once.

You are a *professional*. Your weapon, a steel knife. You strike once. Death is instantaneous, swift. The victim doesn't even realize what is happening. That is what it meant to be a *professional*.

But Anupam-da had said, A *take-over* by the *professionals* is on. Not by the Khokas and Tajus. But by them! Butchers!

Finally, he understood what was about to happen. Anupam-da spent exactly 45 minutes with him, trying to explain. Although before going off to the club, before the prize distribution ceremony at the refugee colony school, before embarking on a round of tiresome social duties, Anupam-da, adhering to the rules of yoga, assumed the *shavasana*[2] pose and relaxed for a while, yet now, in a spirit of boundless compassion, he surrendered that very time just for him.

The *professionals* are taking over. C-C-C or Chanchal Charan Chakladar has been doing the rounds, visiting the *professional* hangouts and leaving word, It's time; Shyama-Ma[3] wants blood.

The *professionals* are disciples of Shyama-Ma. In the month of Kartik,[4] on the auspicious moonless night, the *maha-amabasya*, the towering image of Shyama-Ma—her immense breasts, her filmstar face, her figure moulded from Horlicks grain—is worshipped by them with great pomp and splendour. They spend thousands of rupees on crackers and fireworks, build pandals that block the city streets.

The *professionals* have been informed of Shyama-Ma's wishes. Anupam-da said to Sona alias Akhil, A single individual can't resist a collective force, can't resist an organized class. The same with the *profession*. You are alone. They are organized. You have to come to me for help. They can help themselves. You have just one knife. They have . . .

The list of superior weapons makes the killer realize that yes, the *profession* has at last passed into the hands of the *professionals*.

Anupam-da explains, Say, tomorrow X and Y are to be killed. The *professionals* will write up an entire report, send it to the newspapers tonight it-self. The news will be in the morning papers, even before the van can reach the scene of the crime. That's *professional*!

The killer realizes he is defeated. But his face shows no fear at the consequences of that defeat, no despair at the loss of his livelihood, no disappoint-ment at his sudden dismissal. Just that vacant stony gaze, no hint of a smile. Looking at his master. Any-one who'll pay can be his master. He says, What to do, now?

What do you mean? Go! *Enjoy* yourself. *Relax.*

Suddenly the killer realizes, he's in great dan-ger. Perhaps his very life is under threat. Perhaps he is teetering atop the edge of an extremely sharp razor. Because, suddenly, Anupam Mitra, member of every *society* in Calcutta, says, Not a word to any one.

The desperate urge for self-protection had pro-vided Sajad Mandal's ravaged body with fierce courage. The desperate urge for self-protection pulses through every living creature, even the clam as it cowers before the beak of the wading birds. The killer's blood now thrums with a mad cacophony of bells. The fire-brigade's clanging, the siren. The sudden realization, he may not even last the night! That desperate urge for self-protection thus makes him rattle off a stream of lies. I know what you're thinking. Look, I've noted the details of each *case*, which one of them was carried out where and when and at whose orders, whether it was you, Ajit-babu or Nanda Ray. I've put it in a sealed envelope.

What?

I've given it to someone for safe-keeping. *Anything happening to me*, he'll hand it over to Satish Patra.

This kind of treachery from you, Sona?

The same as yours.

Like mine?

Not yet, perhaps. But in the future.

Not yet! What do you think of me?

My thoughts are only but natural, Anupam-da. You're the one who used to say that Sunil was your right-hand man. You'd said then that if that was treachery, then treachery was the natural law of the day. Remember?

Anupam Mitra was badly shaken. But he's an old hand at the game. Never expresses the anger within, the rage that ferments. He says, Be frank, get down to brass tacks.

What am I to do?

Take it easy.

How?

Go away somewhere. Outside Calcutta.

Outside, evening is fast approaching. The smoggy grey evening of a Calcutta trembling in the winter cold. Everything is growing dark as they speak. Beware of the dark. Sona asks, You'll give me a car. Your car. And money.

But, money . . .

Aren't I getting off your back?

Who's got that envelope?

No one you know.

I see!

Anupam Mitra's body is racked by uneasiness, a dull ache. Who is he to trust? Why is he so alone in this world?

So?

Fine! All right. When?

Five a.m., tomorrow.

Where will you go?

Coochbehar.

Why?

What's it to you.

If I need you?

I won't stay in Coochbehar town. Just visit once in a while. I'll give you the address later. If you write there, I'll get the message.

Sona left, then. He knew Anupam Mitra had made certain phone calls, then. His conversation would have been something like this:

No, Taju! *That programme is off.*

Ajit, he has betrayed us.

Nanda, he's left something for Satish Patra . . .

But Anupam Mitra—standing there in his well-furnished room, under the huge Tibetan wall-hanging, guarded by the rows of bookshelves groaning under the weight of his volumes on law—had admitted to himself that Sona was a *professional* after all! The right move at every step. Or else, had Anupam Mitra's earlier plans been carried out, there would have been a huge mess. If the envelope reached Satish Patra, there would have been a tangled knot indeed. Satish Patra would not be involved in even one of those *cases*. But he would have used Sona's report as his lethal weapon at one time or another. He would have given Sona his reassurance then, protected him. No, it had not been a mistake to let Sona live.

Sona left and went to the local doctor's. A terrible pain in his ears. Sajad had aimed randomly with that brick, banged up his head badly. His ears have been hurting since then.

The doctor had said, Go to the hospital, Sona. See an ear-specialist.

Why?

It's a bad wound. Might even have burst a hole in your eardrums. Show it now or there'll be trouble later.

Sona realized then that these were bad times indeed. The beginning of his downfall. Proper medical attention meant staying in Calcutta, which he can't do. Perhaps an ear will be permanently damaged, he'll lose his hearing, slowly. And after the beating from Khoka and Taju, both his arms throb painfully at the slightest effort. A glass of water feels like a heavy load. Sona emerged from the doctor's, his brows knit in thought.

Home. The thought of it unleashes a heavy, dull rage inside him, overwhelms him. He can seal off his mind, his thoughts, when he's immersed in the work of his profession. His hands do their work, naturally, habitually. Like the *case* boy then remains a boy no longer, like the parents, the vaccination mark on his arms, the lover, the *dot-pen* in his pocket, the heart's blind yearning to rip out the sun from the sky, to scatter the sparks of life, to reach the rays of light into every home, like all of that which matters no longer but becomes only a *case*, so too does Sona no longer remain the son of his parents then, no longer the dada of his brothers and sisters, the grandson of his ailing, simpleton grandmother, the nephew of his widowed aunt.

His mind is empty then, devoid of the memory of vaccination scars on the arm, the desire to wear *terrycot* and smoke expensive cigarettes, the intense craving for *shol* fish, the dream of buying a Fiat and travelling. Then, helped by skill and practice, his fingers silently touch the spring, plunge the blade deep into the *junction* of the head and the shoulders. Then, he is a model of dexterity. This dexterity, like a disembodied, pristine, incandescent, formless entity ripped out by the scalpel of an omnipotent surgeon, torn out from his other entity of flesh and blood, heart and mind, emotions and sensations.

But when he is home, when he is Sona, Sona-moni, Dada, Sona-da, then he is complete. All his entities coalesce then, and then he feels the anger, the disgust, the sorrow.

The family treats him like a rare gem. All of them, so confident of their right to his earnings that buy black-market rice–clothes–asthma medicines–schoolbooks. It makes him so angry.

A magur fish being cut open is enough for his father to whisper 'Krishna' in pain. His mother feeds rice to the crows. They have never asked how their *Pre-U fail*[5] and unemployed son manages to feed the family. Never asked him, that is, never actually said the words. For in truth they know it all. Or else how can his brother dare to abuse the local residents, extort subscriptions from them, how can his father add an extra potato or two brinjals on to the weighing scale at the market, how can his sister brazenly flaunt her sluttish ways? You think Sona doesn't know how?

But they all play their game of hide-and-seek. They hide, he doesn't seek. And vice versa.

He speaks little, whether at home or elsewhere. He does not realize how abnormal he has become, slowly, over time. Not the slightest urge, deep within, to speak to any one. Goes to the tea-shop every day, sips silently at his tea, reads the papers. Spends days without speaking. Never reads books, never watches films, never eyes the girls. Doesn't have any such normal habits. Although at one time he used to talk, talk a lot. He used to talk then, in those days, as long as Ranjan made him talk. Ranjan knew how to make him talk.

Ranjan was his first *case*. The first lesson in the book.

He met Ranjan's sister on the street, just the other day. Anubha had grown even prettier after her marriage. Where is Ranjan, when will he come back, will he come back at all? His family knows nothing even today. That's the best part about having Sona on the job. He stays silent, his *cases* too don't wag their tongues among the people nor blab their secrets to the newspaper headlines.

Anubha was on her way to a wedding, walking through their *colony*. She recognized Sona, stopped to speak to him. Walked beside Sona for a while.

How are you? What are you doing? Do you go to Bakul's?

Anubha was asking a hundred such questions. Ranjan's sister was unaware that his first lesson was her brother's *case*. The thought did not amuse him.

A grunt now, a nod of the head. Saying almost nothing at all.

Anubha said, You've changed a lot!

How?

Just . . . changed.

Perhaps.

He'd walked away without waiting to say goodbye. The evening before he went to Sajad. He'd gone home early. He'd a train to catch, early next morning.

Now, he's rushing home. The bus, tomorrow at dawn. Home, how the thought depressed him. Yet, he had gone back. Just as some solitary wild beasts are known as loners, Sona too was a loner. Sona knew the advantages of being a loner. But presenting that same image before the public now seemed to him a disadvantage. A distinct disadvantage. Because he is no longer the same. His hearing is affected, his elbows hurt, render his arms dangerously ineffectual at times. Besides, Anupam Mitra might initiate some steps against him any minute now if he believed the lies that Sona had fed him.

So, back home, Sona'd asked for some hot water, taken a bath. No one in his family spoke to him, ever. Avoided him. He'd asked for his food, enjoyed his meal. Then packed his things into a small bag. His shirts and trousers were equipped with deep pockets. He'd slid his knife and money into them. Then sent word to Nalin. Through his younger brother. Said, Ask him to bring the car.

The desperate urge for self-protection beats within the killer too just as in everyone else. Sometimes that urge places a small hourglass right in the centre of the heart's lotus. The grains fall with a whisper, keep falling. The trickle of sand, the passing of time. The blood vessels of the heart slowly covered with sand. Sona thus buries the flower, petal by petal, beneath the dripping sand, and sends word to Nalin. Not believing even the word of Anupam Mitra.

Nor in Nalin. Nalin drives his own taxi. The taxi had been arranged for by Nanda Ray. But the city streets are no longer safe for taxis, late at night. So Nalin comes home as soon as its dusk and lies in bed, a small radio clutched to his chest.

Sona made Nalin sleep in his room, that night.

What's the *case*, Sona-da?

Shut up.

He'd been in bed, Nalin on the floor. His widowed aunt glanced at him once, once at Nalin, and then made her bed, hugging the other end of the wall.

Sona watched his aunt fall asleep, Nalin too. Didn't sleep himself, just sat there in the darkness. He was used to staying awake. His profession demanded that he be used to all sorts of things. Or else he'd be in trouble. He woke up Nalin when the clock struck four. The *professionals* were taking over. Out of the house, he instructed Nalin, *Highway*.

Taking no risks whatsoever he went to Ranaghat and boarded the bus. When Anupam

Mitra heard that Sona had left the city, he was voluble in his praise. Sona is a real *professional*! Such unerring professional wisdom, hardened in the very marrow of a man's bones, can be either acquired or inherited. How much of it had Sona acquired, how much ran in his blood? Anupam made a mental note. When the need arose, it was safer to trust a man like Sona. His other trainees couldn't hold a candle to Sona. Butchers! Barbarians!

Thus Sona left Calcutta.

The picture of Sona that remains etched in Anupam Mitra's mind is of a young man with a face much older than his years. Five feet eleven inches tall. At first glance he looks thin, but that wiry body is strong, tough. Medium-length hair, an ordinary cut. Straight eyebrows. Vacant eyes, blank as a white-washed wall. The young man shaves every day, clean, careful, but his cheeks are rough, still. The sensitive skin on his face roughened by the onslaught of experience within an extremely short time. The young man never smiles. Speaks softly. But in an immensely self-confident manner. This confidence stems from the use of his right hand, from its competent functioning. The young man encourages trust, inspires fear.

2

The outward appearance of the man on his way back to Calcutta still fits the above description. But somewhere in the slant of his mouth is the lack of self-confidence. A worried look in his eyes every now and then. No longer as powerful as he used to be. Knows it. It is doubtful whether his hands will always obey his commands. At least this much is certain, they have never regained their old strength.

Hard of hearing. But he doesn't let anyone know. Has mastered the art of lip-reading with the greatest of difficulty. But the really terrifying change lies deep, deep within, where he has grown afraid, lost courage. Only he knows, he is no longer as able as he used to be. The others think he is still strong, still the same. That's what scares him. If he fails at this job (he has no doubt about the reason for his summons), the *professionals* will not fail to put him in his place.

He does not realize how helpless he has grown for he cannot even keep alert these days when necessary. He does not know that the young boy dozing in the seat behind him in the bus has also been summoned by Anupam Mitra.

The young boy's not of his calibre. For purely personal reasons, for mucking about with Anupam's current favourite Basanti in an unnecessarily intimate manner, this young man had been at the receiving end of Anupam's ire. The young man's impressive *record* had not helped to earn him Anupam's forgiveness. The fear of Anupam had made him flee Calcutta, and the fear of the man he'd never seen—Sona.

But Calcutta ran in his blood. He'd glance at newspaper headlines from a distance, and realize how deprived he was of Calcutta—of Goddess Saraswatis woven out of a single ball of twine, of the latest Bombay filmstar numbers at the Lake Maidan every morning, of the Hindi films running in every Chowringhee cinema hall, of the myriad entertainments that the city had on sale.

By then, Basanti reduced to whoring on the street, Anupam was somewhat appeased. He instructed the young man, Keep following Sona. He's arriving on the third. His *case* is on the fourth. And on the fifth you'll . . . That was the only condition laid upon the young man's return to the city.

Anupam didn't forget to send him Sona's picture. The young boy was quite astonished. This was Sona? But he'd seen this face so often. Hang on! Wasn't he with Rani for a few months . . . he could've finished him off then and there, in the Sukhapokhri jungle itself . . . ? But Anupam Mitra hadn't paid attention to any of that. It was essential that Sona come to Calcutta. A crucial job. A job that could only be executed by a loner *professional*. Sona was an *expert*. A hardened *professional*. The young boy listened carefully to all of this, calmed down. The Sukhapokhri jungles were to his advantage. But the power-of-the-youth always yielded before the wishes and the advantages of Anupam Mitra.

The young boy in the bus is asleep. While being transported to Calcutta in the bus, Sona suddenly

felt the nerve at the back of his neck prickle in warning. A look over his shoulder revealed nothing sus-
picious. The nerve, its duty done, went back to sleep.
Almost there now. Passing through Barasat. Barasat.
He'd come to Barasat with Ranjan once, in their
schooldays. To Ranjan's aunt.

They'd eaten large koi fish, rice pudding.

Now, remembering Ranjan, the glare of the
midday sun disappears before his eyes as a *flashback*
flickers across his mind's screen. A moonlit night. A
vast field. In the distance, the rows of trees around
the maidan. The field is rugged, uneven. Far away,
the huge tank. Ranjan and he are walking. His left
arm around Ranjan's shoulders.

You don't know, Sona. You won't understand
even if I tell you.

Tell me.

This victory of ours, will any good come of it?

You're saying it'll do harm instead?

I don't know . . . who knows any longer what's
good and what's not . . . I was just saying . . .

Told anyone you're coming here?

Why should I? I don't tell anything to anyone any longer.

The moonlight. The warm summer breeze. The ruts and grooves of the field gleaming silver, like oft-seen pictures of the surface of the moon. The billion-year-old moon. Sona and Ranjan too were slowly walking backwards, into the past of prehistory. Retreating thus, one can at a point reach a moment in time measurable only in light years. Eternal, unlimited, boundless time. Ranjan had not known that he was crossing the bounds of the present, stepping into the realm of the infinite.

Don't your folks ask?

Why should they? They don't ask me anything these days.

Not a soul here, seen that?

No one stays out late these days.

Ranjan had laughed, softly. There was something he was about to say. Sona shoved hard against his shoulder. Ranjan stumbled, fell down. At that very moment, at the juncture of his head and shoulder, Sona plunged his . . . Death was instantaneous. Yet Sona waited for a while. Earlier in the evening, he'd already hidden a sack, a large rock, some rope, in a ditch near the tank. Then, into the waters. Sona, walking away after the bubbles disappeared, suddenly stumbled. Bent double, began to vomit. Lay there on the field for some time. The smell of shit. The warm summer breeze.

That day, just as he wiped out the existence of Ranjan, so too Sona wiped out a part of his own self, killing it himself, betraying it treacherously, without warning. Ranjan's case was an experiment, a *test case*. He passed the *test*.

Anupam's room. Anupam, Nanda, Ajit.

Over?

Yes.

Any trouble . . .

None.

Good. Now what?

Home. Sleep.

Sona yawns hugely, making his jaws ache. An act. They are watching, waiting for a reaction. Sona gives nothing away.

The desired effect is evident. Fear and admiration in the eyes of all three different-sized middle-aged men. Sona's stony gaze strips them naked, one by one. It is extremely humiliating to be stripped naked thus at this age. The veneer of these years hides the scars of many failures. Only when Sona looks away does Nanda Roy say, Go, now.

Emerging from Anupam's room, strewn with the trophies of his grandfather's tiger hunts, Sona realizes that despite the lack of payment, there have been other gains.

According to the teachings of the Upanishads, he has gained self-realization. Self-knowledge, enlightenment. He has realized that he is a killer. That is his true identity.

3

The bus enters the outskirts of Calcutta. Afternoon. The warm summer breeze. Approaching Beliaghata.

The bus has no option but to slow down. Along the road, flies alight on the lips of dozing shopkeepers. The *montage* rolls on, across Sona's mental screen, the *montage* continues. A documentary film. A sequence of stills arranged one after another by some unknown filmmaker. Sona takes out a mirror from his pocket, checks his face. How terribly old it's grown. Rami, the widowed sister of the Bharsuta tea-stall owner, thinks it's been caused by a lack of love, care and affection.

Rami doesn't know that he will never laugh again, that he will always speak as little as possible. That he will never again lay a wager with a friend to walk all the way to Shyambazar, the north end of the city, after watching a film at the other end in Tollygunge. That he and his friend will never buy slippers off the pavement together, never walk away wearing each other's pair. That he will never take his friend up on a dare, never walk up to a completely unfamiliar woman and ask, Aren't you Nanda? How are you? Waiting for Barun?

Had that part of his old entity still been alive it
would have allowed him to perhaps develop this
youthful streak into its more mature version, but that
part of him was dead, killed by his own hand. Although a killer cannot become a killer all on his own.
He has to be employed. The moment Anupam employed Sona as a killer, that was the very same moment when Sona killed his old, natural self. Shoved
it hard against the shoulders, flung it to the ground.
Then, a touch of the fingers. The spring-knife blade
free, erect, ecstatic, firm young breasts spilling out
under the moonlight. He was the one to plunge the
knife into his natural self, her blade penetrating deep
into the point where its head met its shoulder. The
lusty young blade slid out then with a sigh of satis-
faction. Wiped clean in the dirt. The blade then fell
asleep, comfortable, languid, content after the rush
of her outburst. Sona stuffed his natural self into a
sack. Filled it with large rocks. Tied it with rope. The
corpse of his natural self slid into the sack with the
greatest of ease. The body still warm, soft, pliant.
Crumpled, inside the sack. The knot of the rope.

The splash of the waters. Then bubbles, bubbles, bubbles. Stop. Full stop.

Thus he will never laugh again. Never yield to any of Rami's countless pleas and say, I love you. He will not draw away when Rami embraces his prickly-heat covered, ungratified yet aroused body. But his eyes will remain vacant, expressionless. Not a word of love will spill from those lips.

But Rami is foolish, foolish. She'll say, over and over again, Come back, soon. We'll get married. Promise? Why don't you speak?

Leaving everything with you.

Promise?

The money's here too.

What sort of a heartless brute are you? How my heart hurts just to think of it. Don't know why the hell I bother.

I never asked you to.

So? Burning with fever, you were, then. You think that Bharat Kaola would have looked after you? He's a monster. That tiny ramshackle hut, only a heap of bamboo slats, and look at the rent he made you pay? Do you know how much he earns through those huts of his?

He wasn't supposed to look after me.

But isn't he human?

Never mind him.

Curse the day I heard you moaning, went to feed you barley-water. Never could ignore the suffering of the sick. My husband had a chronic cough, rheumatism. Thirteen when I married, how I nursed him, do you know? He'd another wife. Never lifted a finger. She'd had a son, that was enough, she'd no need to do any more.

Does it hurt?

What?

The thought of him?

Why the hell for?! Just about fifteen and I was a widow. Never knew what 'husband' meant. How could I? When I married, the other one'd two kids already. They got me for their odd jobs, run around all day with rice and water, shabu and sugar, warm oil and garlic.

When was that?

Must be some ten years ago. Since then, I've never been able to ignore anyone's suffering. And that's what'll be the death of me. Dada says . . .

What?

He says that you're not the Shyam Sha'u-Chan'an Goldar type. You're a bhadralok.

Is that so?

He says you've dropped in all of sudden, and you'll leave the same way too.

I will. But I'll come back.

Promise?

I will.

Marry me?

Let's see.

Or is it fixed up already? That's why you're in such a hurry to leave?

No.

He will not go back to Rami. The principal and primary reason being that after the job's done, the old place may not be safe for him any longer. Then

again he thinks that with his broken body, it may not
be a bad idea for him and Rami to go away, further
north, to set up a tea-stall, spend the rest of his life
there. Rami's the one who runs her dada's tea-stall.
The brother makes the tea. Rami fries eggs, makes
potato chops, toasts bread. Serves the customers.

Rami knows the customers, talks to them.
There you are Netai-da! The wife back yet? . . . How
long will you hang about over those two cups of tea?
Go on, go home. . . . Schoolgirls skipping classes for
a cup of tea, what next, I ask you!

Rami, garrulous, sharp-tongued. Many people
hate her bossy manner, but she has grown up in
these parts. Knows all the secrets. The locals are
wary of her, she'll spill the beans, make a noise if
she gets angry.

They're also scared because the money from
the sale of the potato chops is all her own. She in-
vests that money in the money-lending business. Almost everyone here now owes her some. She never
waives the interest. But keeps the rates low.

If he and Rami go away, set up that tea-stall, life would carry on after a fashion. The way his body was crumbling, some amount of tender loving care might even help him stay well. But the little money that he's left with is not enough to start a tea-stall. He wouldn't have decided to return to Calcutta had he not fallen short of cash.

The thought of Calcutta fills him with fear. Fear of the unknown. The *professionals* have taken over. What are they like? Are they still devotees of Shyama-Ma? This year too they'd organized an idol made entirely from baby-food powder, but were they still devotees? Who knew?

Sona is alone. They are organized, functioning according to a well-planned programme. Why the summons for Sona then, even after their *take-over*? Sona knows only too well the convoluted workings of Anupam Mitra's mind. For certain, this time, for some reason or the other, the *professionals* had refused the *case*. If so, then the *case* must be a very important one. Who is the *case*?

Sona just cannot figure it out. Away from the capital for some time now, the map of current events is unknown to him. Who is planning what, how are the events being organized, what is happening where—he knows nothing. He'd never wanted to know, even in the past. Who's orders, who's the man. That was enough. The payment was fixed. The rates increased according to the risks involved. They never decreased.

The bus is entering Esplanade. A traffic-jam at the Suren Banerjee Road crossing.

The driver pokes his head out, asks, What's up, dada?

Truck's on the footpath.

When?

Just now.

Oh, no hope then.

Twenty minutes, at the very least. Perhaps half an hour, maybe even an hour. Everything seems so complicated to Sona. So many people talking, so much being said. Was it possible to understand everything just by lip-reading? A faint web of sound whispers at his ears. So hard, so hard to catch.

So hard not being able to hear. How long can he stay in Calcutta? Can he get his ears checked? If the doctor asks him to buy a hearing aid? That's a big blow, a thousand at one go. If he spends it on the hearing aid, will there be enough for the tea-stall?

Thinking about his hearing makes his head ache, his ears hurt. Rami'd tried, dipped a paan stem in warm oil and let it drip, drop by drop, into his ears, but it hadn't helped. Rami'd mentioned some witch doctor. The man she bought her potatoes from, Chhediram Bhakat, he was an expert at driving out evil spirits. Sona hadn't paid her any attention. Rami'd lost her temper. Bhadralok-babu's got a bhadralok ailment! Only a *daktar*[6] will do for him!

That last *case*. Sajad Mandal. That unexpected attack and since then, his ear's a mess. Now, sitting in the bus rendered still by the traffic-jam, Sona began to remember it all.

He'd taken a bus from Canning station. Got off, then walked to Sajad's village. The lie had been necessary. He was on the run, seeking shelter. Sajad was known in those parts as eccentric, mad. A wizened man, a sharecropper. But he still hadn't mastered the art of suffering a beating silently. He also had a soft corner for those on the run. Besides, he was currently the only obstacle in the way of Ishwar Sanpui who wanted Sajad's few bighas, in order to build a fishery. It was only because of Sajad that Ishwar couldn't flood that patch of cultivable land, couldn't embark upon the fish trade for the benefit of the common masses.

Sona was surprised when he was offered more than the usual for the job. He hadn't known Sajad's background. Hadn't wanted to know. More money meant more responsibilities. The village was in the interiors of Canning. Escaping would be risky. But this was the first time that arrangements were made for his return, from Canning. In a truck carrying rice. Although the stretch from the village to Canning would have to be done at his own risk. Sajad thus was important because of all these reasons. But Sajad's nature had been to Sona's advantage. There was not a single influential character in those parts whom Sajad had not antagonized.

He had reached Sajad's village in the afternoon. He spent the whole day lying down, inside the thatched hut. Sajad himself drew water from the muddy pond for his use. He'd eaten stale rice in water, snail-curry and spinach for lunch. Then lain down wordlessly on a tattered and smelly straw mat.

At night, after his meal made of little bits of grain and *khesari* pulses, he'd complained of stomach cramps. Sajad had helped him to the edge of the pond, carrying a lamp to light the way. Sona hadn't known that Sajad's knees were not rheumatic in the slightest, hadn't known that Sajad never leaned forward, his knees bent. Hadn't taken note of Sajad's bone-structure in the light of day. It would have helped him had he done so.

As a result Sona suffered a severe beating. Sajad had kept hitting him with chunks of brick. The only saving grace, at least Sajad wasn't screaming. Just hissing in the dark, Been paid to kill, you traitor, to kill?

Sajad was a fool. Why should Sona kill unless he was paid for it? Sona hadn't anticipated such a reaction from Sajad. He'd slipped in the mud, fallen down. Sona'd then ground Sajad's face into the mud with his hands. Sajad began contorting his body, trying to slip free. Kept hurling bricks at Sona, blindly, randomly. Sona'd fallen down, then. And Sajad pounded away madly at his head, near his ears.

Only by overcoming that terrible agony had Sona completed his job.

He had not forgotten Sajad.

The bus began to move. Sona checked to see where he'd kept his bag.

The boy in the seat behind him brushed a lock of hair from his forehead. Now he didn't have to follow Sona any more. Anupam Mitra would instruct him about his next duty.

Sona got into a taxi.

The boy emerged from the bus terminus, began to look around for a telephone.

4

Anupam Mitra put an end to the discussion, As of now, Satish Patra is *out*! Satish has been stirring up too much trouble, investigate this, investigate that. Sheltering discontents, defectors from Anupam's gang. Certainly not out of charity alone. If Anupam Mitra doesn't do a thing to protect his own boys, what's that to you? He's apparently also appointed three people, just to record confessions in short-hand, keep *records*. Those confessions were the bases of the *case* being constructed against Anupam, Nanda Ray and Ajit-babu.

The thing is, Anupam Mitra explains, Never trust anyone. You're being chased out, can't seek shelter, all right. But to lose all sense of loyalty?

It's being lost after all, it seems, says Nanda Ray.

Ajit-babu is a recent devotee of Anahari Baba. Baba's teachings are bringing him round to the opinion that these methods were all wrong. Mars has finally moved away. His Jupiter was in the ascendant. The next eighteen years in his life, a veritable golden age. Baba had assured him. The Baba is an MA, has a Law degree. Young. Speaks French and Sindhi. The new-and-improved Bhrigu[7] in astrological circles. His powers of prediction arming Ajit-babu with immense self-confidence.

Ajit-babu says, Why not do a *mutual* with him?

No.

It's very easy for you to say no.

And for you to say nothing.

The two middle-aged men glare ferociously at each other.

Nanda Ray says, Anupam is right.

How?

It'll be a *double* job. Satish Patra gone. *No more fear*!

The *records*?

His typists have already been spoken to . . . *Really* Ajit! You're not paying them and neither am I. Anupam's the one who . . .

Of course he's paying. He's the one who's stuck the worst!

He's paying. *No Satish Patra. You get the records.* Then, those who've *betrayed* us will be shaking in their shoes. They'll figure out what's best, return to the fold.

Will they?

Of course! Anupam Mitra smashes a flabby, spongy fist into an equally flabby, spongy palm.

I tell you today . . . Nanda Ray, as though addressing the country's countless millions, things should not have come to this. But now we have no choice.

Why? Have arrangements been made already?

Anupam looks up, *Come in, Sona!*

Sona comes in. Looks at all of them. Then looks at Anupam.

Ajit-babu says, I'm off.

Yes. You go, Nanda, you too. *By the by*, Ajit, you're not going alone. Khoka and Taju are going too. They're staying at your place.

What do you mean?

You may try something funny.

Who says so?

I know you. They'll spend the night in the room that has the telephone. Don't misunderstand me, Ajit.

At home? What do I say?

When you take home whores, what do you say then?

Keep one thing in mind.

What?

It'll get out of hand. There'll be arrests.

Anupam Mitra's shoulders moved in a typical 'barrister' shrug. He said, *Frankly*, Ajit, after all that's happened, I can't imagine what sort of *reaction* there'll be now.

Why worry? None of us will talk.

Really?

Ajit and Nanda left.

ANUPAM MITRA LOOKED AT SONA. No. Looks all right. Looks trustworthy. Who cares if he's not, anyway. Sona won't make it past the evening of the fifth. Just the thought of it, so painful. Anupam is no ordinary man. Travelled all over the world. Just for the sake of leaving no witnesses he has to sacrifice such a wonderful *professional* at the hands of some *crude barbarian*. Feeding his thousand-rupee flower bed to a five-rupee goat. Destroying an ancient sculpture with a chisel. Oh, how intolerable, life's inevitable barbarities! How heartbroken he'd been when he'd visited the caves of Ajanta as a young man and found the priceless paintings scratched over by vandals.

But what other choice has he? His ancestors had erected their palaces on the banks of the Red River, then built secret storerooms within. They'd had to kill the artisans, have them trampled upon by elephants. What to do, can't let there be witnesses, see? If there'd been some other way, then . . . ?

He has to be free now, free of the tangled net. Now, before him, lies a world of opportunity. A great world, beckoning. Thus Satish . . . thus Sona . . .

Sona asks, Who?

Satish Patra?

How?

He comes this way, Saturdays and Tuesdays. His garden house is behind the factory.

I know.

The factory's having a lockout.

Oh.

Just before dark. You'll be inside the room. The gardener will let you in.

The *driver*?

Spoken to. He'll be away. Step out for a cup of tea. The gardener'll leave for the market.

All right.

One thing—*I want him to be discovered.*

All right!

You'll get five.

Eight.

Thousand?

What did you think, lakhs?

Too much.

Then forget it.

Okay. Agreed.

One thing—I want to have a look around to-morrow morning.

Take my car. Drive it slowly. Don't get down.

My *protection*?

You'll get it. Are you having trouble hearing?

Why?

Looks like you're lip-reading.

Why?

Just . . . thought.

No.

All right then.

Sona left. Sweat, cold sweat. The bastard had caught on all right. Thank God, Sona hadn't asked for a glass of water. A large glass was all it would have taken. What if his hands had begun to tremble?

The cold sweat, still. Satish Patra! Good god!

Husband to Anupam's cousin. Satish Patra. A Very Important Person. Calcutta will burn again.

Sona left, the boy from the bus stepped in. Anupam said, You're staying here.

Yes, sir.

Don't try to leave.

No, sir.

Anupam rang the bell. Asked for his car. Now he has a speech to deliver, 'On the Baul Tradition', at a music festival. Now he has nothing to worry about.

Not Ajit-babu, but Nanda Ray, rushing to the bathroom the moment he reached home. Filled up the *bathtub*. Lay down in it, a baby in his mother's lap. Then lifted the telephone tucked into a secret niche in the wall. Must warn Satish Patra. Anupam had gone stark staring mad. But Nanda Ray can't afford any risks now, not when Patra's helping him to bag such a major *contract*.

Anupam Mitra finished his speech, went to New Market.[8] Satish Patra's wife Bula is so fond of roses. She was a great fan of Anupam's. The thought of Satish Patra is sad, true. But he's got no choice. Satish will be at the club. That's why Anupam's come, now. This too will go on *record*—that on the eve of the incident, he dropped in at their house on a social visit. Bula'll be the one to say so. Speaking through her tears. He felt like buying some cake. But he restrained himself. Not a child in that house, who's the cake for? Satish Patra has no children. And Bula keeps changing godmen. Is it any wonder that Satish is going from mad to worse, these days? Had he any children, he would have been a normal person like Anupam. A father, a compassionate friend. Anupam bought all the roses in the shop.

Meanwhile, Ajit-babu watched Taju and Khoka as they polished off the chicken curry at his table, relaxed, sitting with folded feet on his chairs. Dinner over, they asked, Dadu, d'you need to use the bathroom?

Shut up!

Hope you don't have a telephone there.

Taju said, Oh, pipe down. Quit griping.

Still, let me go take a look.

Taju scratched his ears thoughtfully and said, Disconnected two lines already. Who knows which one goes where?

Ajit-babu began to tremble in rage.

Said, I'm going to bed.

Taju said, See you. You must get some hilsa tomorrow. Haven't had some for a long time.

Satish Patra put down the phone. The club phone. Through the operator. Looked at his watch. Whatever Nanda Ray may say, he'll go immediately. A nameless dread, surging within. Sent word to his driver. What does Nanda Ray want to tell him?

Then Nanda Ray and Satish Patra went to Anupam's house. Then Nanda Ray, Satish Patra and Anupam went to Satish Patra's house. Then locked the doors. The crackle of sheet after sheet of paper being torn, the only sound. A long, long time. Night paled into dawn. Satish Patra looked up. Anupam said, You didn't *lose*. We've *gained*.

Hmm.

Now you see, we can work in *coordination*.

But Sona?

Something will be done.

I don't trust you.

You can be there.

Is Nanda asleep?

No, I'm not.

Ajit?

He'll be there too, Satish. Why worry?

Who will do it?

A new chap. You don't know him.

But even he . . . ?

We'll send him away.

What do you mean?

Why do you want to know what I mean?

Can one trust him?

Not like Sona . . . But you know, this has re-
sulted in your *gain*. Those who were coming to you
. . . once they see that you're no longer . . . Yes.

The morning of the fourth, each of them returned to their respective homes. The afternoon of the fourth, having slept soundly, Anupam summoned his current secretary, Surajit. Take down a *report*. For tomorrow's papers.

Yes, sir.

Write: Yesterday evening the police discovered the body of anti-social Akhil alias Sona in the abandoned warehouse of '_____' factory. The body bore marks of knife wounds. The youth . . .

Sir!

Yes?

I saw Sona today. Sitting in the shop, drinking tea.

So what? It's afternoon now. The body is 'discovered' in the evening. Reported in tomorrow's papers. Where's the problem?

Yes sir!

Write: The youth had been for a long time . . .

Surajit began to write.

Anupam finished dictating. Said, Go home.

Yes sir.

Forget about it.

Yes sir.

Surajit left, trembling in fear.

5

Sona is sitting in a room inside the garden house. A
'garden house' in name only. Nothing but a garden.
Puritan Satish Patra has no other interests. The flowers in this garden win prizes every year.

The walls of the room hung with pictures of his
wife Bula's discarded godmen. The lady changes
gurus every other day. Commissions each of their
portraits. Can't bring herself to throw them away.
Brings them here instead.

Hence, the pictures on the wall. Once a year, a
three-night-long kirtan session is arranged at this
house. The lawn covered with a canopy. After the
singing, prasad is distributed. A huge crowd gathers,
not an inch of space.

Sona reaches the place exactly at dusk. The
gardener wordlessly lets him in. An entrance hall in

the front. Two rooms further down. Can be reached through the hallway. Their doors kept open now. Lights in the hall. Sona, sitting behind the heavy curtains. The door behind him is closed. He will leave through that door.

Sona is wearing a spotless white shirt and dhoti. When he leaves, walks down the road, he must look like a respectable young man. There should be no cause for suspicion.

His right hand hurts. Wrenched unexpectedly, at an odd angle, in the bath today. Anyway. Just this one job. This last time.

Sona realizes that there'll be no more jobs after this. He won't let himself be trapped by Anupam Mitra's snares today. Because today he knows, he can't go on any more. He doesn't know why it feels as though, deep within, his old natural self is slowly beginning to draw back the curtains, peel back the veils, open the doors, come out into the open. The same self he had killed with his own hands, light-years ago.

Today, how strange, when he heard that his sister's marriage had been arranged, he'd broken into a smile. Astonishing his mother to such a degree that the bowl of dal almost fell from her hands.

They want a lot. At least three thousand.

He'll give it. Eight thousand minus three thousand still leaves five. About a thousand to set up the tea-stall. The rest he'll give to Rami. Rami'll loan it out with interest. They'll get by.

Take this, this plan to unite his future with Rami's, what did this mean? Was his natural self conducting a *take-over* of his present self?

But every kill is not a killing. The dead do not always die. They are born again, they live once again, in memory, in the desire to be normal, natural, if only to be loved. Why had Sona taken so long to realize? By the time he realized, his hands were rendered useless. His ears could hear sounds emitted from a particular corner of the room only, and that too very faintly. Or else, nothing. Just yesterday, the cat knocked over a cup which fell to the floor with a crash. Sona was watching. Sona heard nothing.

Now, his ears are cocked in such a way that he can hear Satish Patra the moment he enters the hall.

Rami may say, Marry me. Perhaps he will. Now, after all this time, the thought, perhaps he shouldn't have heeded Anupam's instructions about Ranjan. Perhaps he should have escaped, instead.

Sona shakes his head. He couldn't have escaped. Escape was not possible. Anupam wouldn't have let him. This relationship with that man was destined, fated.

Sona used to fight, one gang to another, for money, *nylon* shirts, even cigarettes.

He'd scoff at idealism, spit in the face of morality. Sona was the kind of person who knew in his gut, in his blood, that those words were mere lies, trickery, only little bits of silver wrapping, look, empty inside, no lozenge!

If he got the money he did the job. Never whipped himself up into a frenzy before a fight, never abused his opponent. He'd just say, It's nothing personal.

Only Sona had the courage to take his victim to the doctor, afterwards, to the hospital. Hence the fanatics, those young men who were drunk on ideology, they didn't trust him. Sells himself, they'd say, dripping disgust. Sona used to tell them, You're sold too. Just don't know it yet.

Ranjan understood Sona. He'd laugh. Say, You're such a pest!

Worm or scorpion?

Scorpion of course!

Sona'd laughed too, then. Laughed while his slippers got exchanged with Ranjan's, laughed while walking with him from Shyambazar to Tollygunge, he'd laughed then, laughed along with Ranjan. Ranjan knew what he was, accepted who he was and yet remained friends, hence he had gifted Ranjan a space close to his heart. He'd never scoffed at Ranjan's ideals. Because Ranjan made no mention of them in his presence.

Ranjan would stand with him on the street corner, eye the girls, browse through the newspapers, go to the cinema. Not a single Hindi film that they hadn't watched together. All-night concerts in the neighbourhood, and the two of them huddled on the front steps of some house, as close to the stage as possible, listening, together.

Every one used to say, Can't trust that Sona. No pride in his homeland whatsoever. Sona'd say, Just because Baba's a *bangal*[9] from East Pakistan doesn't mean I'm one too. This is my homeland, this Calcutta. What's it got to be proud of? Bloody treacherous hole!

He'd tell his father, Yes, yes, so you're used to forty pieces of hilsa for two rupees only. So? What's it to me? Homeland? *Desh*? What the hell's that?

This was Sona. Why was this Sona discovered by Anupam Mitra?

Why, one day during that terrible, anarchic, violent, dark decade, did Anupam come home, asking for him?

No. Sona could not have escaped, then. Perhaps he will marry Rami. But there'd already been a marriage, a long time ago, between his professional skill and Anupam's gut for talent. Destined. Fated. Marriages after all are made in heaven.

But this time Sona will escape. From Calcutta, from Anupam's clutches, from everything. To hell with all those carefully nurtured dreams of the past. Who wants to go around the city in a Fiat, to sport long sideburns and puff away at expensive cigarettes, to flaunt a pocketful of ten-rupee notes? Sona is going away now, surrendering all that of his own free will.

Sona will go away, some obscure town, a small marketplace. Just one bus that comes and goes. A small tea-stall, a fence around it, tiles on the roof. The fence, plastered with mud. The kitchen, large. Or else the heat from the clay oven will be too much for Rami frying her potato chops. Some pictures, a calendar, on the wall. The small radio on Sona's table. Sona'll sit at the *cash*.

They'll live in a room behind the shop. Their cot, its legs placed on bricks. Underneath, they'll store things for the shop, eggs, tea, sugar.

If the tea-stall works, Sona will set up a *hotel*, serve rice-meals. In small roadside marketplaces, along the routes travelled by private or government buses, such little *hotels* make good money. Roaring trade. Sona has seen many of them.

Rami'll work as long as her body permits. Sona in any case will have to employ an extra hand. Later, perhaps, Sona can send for that *loafer* brother of his.

Sona will buy a sari tonight itself. Rami will be happiest if he leaves tomorrow, on the early-morning bus itself. She won't believe her eyes. Rami's glowing face, her astonished smile, Sona can see it all in his mind's eye.

That face, captured in a *freeze-shot* in his mind. He kept looking, looking at Rami's face, her glowing face, the smile on that face. The freezing picture prepared itself to remain thus for eternity, for so many light-years to come. The time of the picture's stillness now even beyond light-years, now running towards endless, boundless time, now rushing across the borders of the finite, now speeding towards the realm of the infinite, hurtling towards the Time before time itself.

Sona sits there, staring in front.

Outside, on the road behind the house, a car stops. Sona hears nothing. Nor does he hear the sound of several pairs of shoes walking across the garden. The door, the back door, behind him, opens quietly.

Four middle-aged men enter, stand close, their backs against the wall. Sona's co-passenger in the bus, the young boy, moves towards Sona. Sona hears nothing. Doesn't have a clue. Just sits there, staring at the front.

The boy comes near Sona. A knife in his hand. The four men at the back, still, unmoving.

True killers don't need the knife.

Translator's Notes

I

Fisherman

1 Hindu low-caste; untouchables who burn the dead and tend to the cremation grounds.

2 Roll of tobacco enclosed in a leaf for smoking; cheap, indigenous smoke.

3 Literally 'three-eyed'; a mark on the fish's head giving it a three-eyed appearance.

4 Colloquial Bengali pronunciation of 'partner'.

5 Tarakeshwar is a pilgrimage spot in West Bengal, well known for its Shiva temple where devotees congregate once a year, during the full moon in Sraban, the Bengali month corresponding to July–August.

6 'Bhadralok' refers to a social category in Bengal which embraces different strata of upper- and middle-income groups, landed interests as well as administrative employees and professionals, marked out by common standards of 'respectable' behaviour and cultural norms. The outward manifestations of the bhadralok (to which members of the group had to rigorously conform), made possible by a basic standard of income, were (i) residence in a 'pucca' house,

either through ownership or renting; (ii) attention to one's sartorial style in public; (iii) use of a chaste Bengali that was being shaped from the middle of the nineteenth century; and (iv) a noticeable knowledge of English language and manners.

With the rise of the professional middle class— government officials, lawyers, teachers, doctors etc.— the term 'babu' came to be used as a Bengali version of the English 'mister' or 'sir'. The babu in fact had been a perennial butt of ridicule in the farces written by the bhadraloks through the nineteenth century. The term was also used sometimes in a sense of respect (when attached as a prefix to the names of rich banias or businessmen, as distinct from 'raja/maharaja' used for the richer aristocratic landowners) and sometimes in a pejorative sense to describe the parvenu. [See Sumanta Banerjee, *The Parlour and the Streets: Elite and Popular Culture in Nineteenth Century Calcutta* (Calcutta: Seagull Books, 1998).]

7 A traditional hand-woven towel used variously, e.g. to tie things up into a bundle, or as a multipurpose handkerchief used by village folk to wipe off perspiration, to tie about the forehead as a protection against the sun, etc.

II.

Knife

1   Colloquial Bengali pronunciation of 'public'.

2   Title for an astrologer whose predictions have earned
    him fame.

3   Month in the Bengali calendar corresponding to
    May–June.

4   Bitter herb.

5   Dish prepared with bitter gourd and other nutritious
    vegetables.

6   Fish of the eel variety which, apart from its distinctive
    delicious taste, is considered to have therapeutic value
    for patients.

7   Bagha Jatin was the name by which the famous rev-
    olutionary Jatindranath Mukhopadhyay (1880–1915)
    was known in Bengal. He died fighting the British
    forces near Balasore in Orissa in September 1915.
    Ashananda Dhenki is a freedom-fighter invented by
    the author for this particular story.

8   Prayer to the Ganga, asking for the life (of the new
    police thana, in this case) to be made eternal.

9   Colloquial Bengali pronunciation of 'blue films'.

10 Announced by Indira Gandhi during the 1975 Emer-
    gency which, while pretending to be populist, inau-
    gurated a witch-hunt on her political opponents and
    oppression upon the common people.

11 Literally 'god of prem'/'god of love'; colloquial for
    the name assumed by a local godman.

12 Colloquial for 'Kamakshya-tantra', a popular erotic
    treatise harking back to Kamakshya, Assam, vener-
    ated both as a pilgrimage site and a centre of religio-
    sexual practices.

13 Types of cheap paperbacks popular among semi-
    literate readers. While *Grihasth-er Totka* dealt with quick
    remedies for common ailments, *Master–Chhatri Katha*
    (Story of a Teacher and His Girl-student) and *Kamini
    Kaaman Daagey* (The Woman Firing Her Cannon) were
    obviously, as their titles indicate, erotic stories.

14 Literally, 'life'; also used as a term of endearment.

15 Hindi term for 'wedding'.

16 Colloquial Bengali pronunciation of 'border'.

17 Term used by members of political groups and anti-
    social gangs in West Bengal to describe an act of vi-
    olence undertaken by them in retaliation against their
    foes. An *action-master* is one who is an expert in un-
    dertaking such actions.

18 Or Writers' Building, headquarters of the West Bengal government in Calcutta, still carrying the name by which the administrative office of the East India Company was known in the past when the Company's clerks or 'writers' worked there.

19 Here slang for 'boss' or 'chief'.

20 Colloquial Bengali pronunciation for 'protection'. Like 'P'em-er Thakur', the syllable 'r' is often slurred over by the lumpen Bengalis in their conversation.

21 Gauribari: a locality in the north-eastern end of Calcutta where, in the early 1980s, the citizens grew frustrated with police inaction against a local gang lord and rose in revolt, driving him out from the area. Gauribari thus became a symbol of popular resistance against gangsters who were patronized by politicians. Anantapur is the name of the small town described in this story.

22 Educated Bengali political leaders and their followers who took part in the anti-imperialist national movement in the pre-Independence era.

23 Sycophants, toadies or hangers-on.

24 Long periods of daily failure in the electricity supply to Calcutta and the suburbs.

III.

Body

1 A popular shopping area in south Calcutta.

2 A settlement of refugees from East Pakistan (now Bangladesh), who after the 1947 partition of the sub-continent migrated to West Bengal, occupied vacant lands in towns and suburbs, and built makeshift dwellings.

3 King of Magadha in the fifth century BC.

4 Masoor dal and turmeric are believed to be 'Raja-sic'—possessing the Rajas Guna or energy. Traditionally, widows were to lead a life of abstinence, avoiding (among other things) Rajasic food that is considered to possess aphrodisiac powers and to generate creative, passionate and frenetic energy.

5 Another name of Arjuna, the hero of the Mahabharata, meaning 'ambidextrous'.

IV.

Killer

1 Ballpoint pen.

2 A pose in yogic exercises where the practitioner lies supine like a *shava* or dead person.

3 Another name for Goddess Kali.

4 Month in the Bengali calendar corresponding to October–November.

5 Pre-University; equivalent to the Higher Secondary examinations.

6 Doctor; here referring to a registered medical practitioner.

7 Ancient sage, renowned for his accurate mapping of the incidents of human life through posterity.

8 A sprawling fashionable marketplace behind Chowringhee in Calcutta, well known for, among other things, its flower shops.

9 A term used usually in a derogatory sense by certain people from West Bengal to describe those coming from East Bengal (now Bangladesh) and their dialect.